EVOLUTION™

EVOLUTION™

Written by Eleanor Fremont

Story by Don Jakoby and
David Diamond & David Weissman

Screenplay by David Diamond & David Weissman

PUFFIN BOOKS

Published by the Penguin Group

Penguin Putnam Books for Young Readers,

345 Hudson Street, New York, New York 10014, U.S.A.

Penguin Books Ltd, 27 Wrights Lane, London W8 5TZ, England

Penguin Books Australia Ltd, Ringwood, Victoria, Australia

Penguin Books Canada Ltd, 10 Alcorn Avenue, Toronto, Ontario, Canada M4V 3B2

Penguin Books (N.Z.) Ltd, 182-190 Wairau Road, Auckland 10, New Zealand

Penguin Books Ltd, Registered Offices: Harmondsworth, Middlesex, England

Published by Puffin Books,

a division of Penguin Putnam Books for Young Readers, 2001

1 3 5 7 9 10 8 6 4 2

TM & © 2001 DreamWorks

Text by Eleanor Fremont
Puffin Books ISBN 0-14-230053-5

Printed in the United States of America

EVOLUTION™

CHAPTER ONE

I t was dark in outer space. Dark and very cold. The meteor hurtled toward Earth, its metallic surface glowing faintly. In the distance, the unsuspecting Earth was bathed in the warmth of the massive sun.

The meteor skimmed across the outer edge of Earth's atmosphere, catching it just enough to alter its course a bit. It arced down toward the surface of the planet. The friction caused the meteor to break apart as it fell.

Most of the pieces burned up as they streaked through the air. But not all of them. A single large piece, as jagged as a great shard of glass, survived intact. It glowed red as it rocketed downward, its point headed straight for the blue planet.

● ● ●

Wayne Gray, like everyone else on Earth, was blissfully unaware of what was happening in the skies above him. It was just before dawn in the Arizona desert, but Wayne was already busy. A young man in his twenties, he wore a dirty white T-shirt and black suspenders. If anyone else had been out in the desert at that hour, they would have observed Wayne struggling to pull something out of the trunk of his old Oldsmobile. The thing was heavy, and he was having a hard time.

It was a body, limp and covered with a blanket. A pants-covered leg hung out from underneath the cloth.

The body was so heavy that Wayne could barely wrestle it out of the trunk. Finally, he got his arms under it and hoisted it all the way out, dropping it to the ground with a *thunk*.

The blanket fell away, uncovering the head and revealing that the thing was, in fact, not a body at all. It was a life-size dummy. Wayne grabbed it by the feet and started dragging it toward an abandoned mining shack that sat in the middle of the desert.

Thump . . . thump . . . thump. The dummy's head bumped against the rocks as Wayne pulled it along. When he reached the shack, he kicked open the door and disappeared inside.

In a few minutes, he emerged without the dummy. He padlocked the door behind him. Then he went back to the car, reached into his trunk, and pulled out a five-gallon can of gasoline. He proceeded to douse the shack with the gas.

". . . and then the fire started," he said aloud. As he said the words, he took out a match and set the shack ablaze. It went up with a *whoosh* that nearly knocked him off his feet.

"It's on!" he yelled, immediately pulling out a large stopwatch and clicking it on with his thumb. With the second hand ticking, he scrambled into a heavy pair of yellow fireman's pants and matching yellow coat. He raced back to the shack, an ax in hand.

"We're going in!" he yelled, going at the door with his ax. *Whack! Whack! Whack!* He threw the ax down, pushed away the splintered wood, and climbed into the burning structure.

In a moment, he emerged from the shack, coughing and gasping, carrying the dummy. "Is there anyone else in the building with you?" he yelled to the dummy as he raced to get clear of the fire. "Squeeze my hand if the answer is yes!" There was no response. He put the dummy down on the ground and started giving it mock mouth-to-mouth resuscitation. "C'mon! C'mon! You gotta fight!" he urged the dummy.

He glanced back over to the blazing shack. "Get those people back!" he yelled to nobody in particular. Then he went back to performing feverish CPR on the dummy. "Breathe, dammit! Breathe!" he commanded desperately.

The dummy was not breathing, but Wayne did not give up. He did more CPR. He tried heart massage. He went back to the mouth-to-mouth. And then, slowly, he smiled, lifting the dummy's head up with great care. She was going to survive!

But then, over the noise of the crackling fire, Wayne heard a sound. It was a sort of whistling noise, not like anything he had ever heard before, and it kept getting louder.

Wayne looked up, and there it was: an enormous fireball

in the sky. It was screaming like a gigantic teapot, and it was heading straight for him.

"What the . . ." said Wayne. He started running, with that terrifying screaming whistle getting louder every second. Faster and faster he raced, as fast as his legs could carry him. But the fireball was getting bigger and bigger, falling faster and faster, glowing bright red. Wayne dove for the ground.

Thwaammm! The earth rocked as the meteor slammed into the shack like a huge dagger and disappeared into the ground. Wayne's Oldsmobile, which had been parked beside the shack, flipped away like a matchstick.

Where the shack had been, there was now nothing but a large hole in the ground. Wayne's car had landed on its side, a good fifty yards from where it had been.

Stunned, Wayne stared at the Oldsmobile. "Drat!" he said.

● ● ●

The Rancho Grande Condominiums was a community of attached gray houses that sat on the outskirts of Glen Canyon, Arizona. In one of these houses, Ira Kane—a tall, good-looking guy in his thirties—found himself being shaken awake by his girlfriend, Denise.

Ira was a smart guy, a guy who was used to being the smartest one in the room. But a big bump in life's road—a bump he didn't really talk about with anyone—had encouraged in him a strong sense of irony. Ira was a cynic. And now, here he was, being shaken awake by a girlfriend with big hair.

"What was that?" Denise was saying.

"What?" Ira responded groggily. "What was what?"

"Did you feel that?" she asked. "Like an earthquake?"

Ira looked around, slowly coming to his senses. It was then that he noticed that a suitcase was standing in the middle of the floor. Clothes were strewn all over the room.

"What are you doing?" Ira inquired.

"I'm leaving you," replied Denise.

Ira raised one eyebrow. Then he looked again at the clothes. "That's my shirt," he said. "And that one."

"For God's sake, Ira, I just told you I was leaving you."

"I gotta say, it looks more like you're robbing me," said Ira.

Denise groaned in disgust.

Ira sat up in bed. "Can I ask you why?" he said.

Denise looked around the condo. It had that look which is sometimes described as "lived-in."

"You live like a guy who just got out of prison," she said. "You teach at a community college, you hang out with that idiot Harry . . ."

"So it's like a combination of things," said Ira drily.

"You don't give a damn about anything," she went on. "I need someone who cares about the world and his place in it. You're going nowhere."

Ira tried to maintain his expression of amused detachment, but the look on his face betrayed his real feeling. That one had actually stung.

"When I first met you," Denise continued, "you were like nobody I'd ever seen in the state of Arizona. I thought you were better than this place." She zipped the suitcase fiercely. "Turns out you're worse," she said. "Good-bye, Ira."

Then she picked up the suitcase and walked out the door, slamming it behind her.

"I want those shirts back!" Ira called after her, having recovered his cynicism.

He looked at the door a moment, and then turned back over and shut his eyes. It would be time to get up and go to work soon.

CHAPTER TWO

Ira taught biology at the local community college, which had a campus that looked more like a corporate park than a university. And so, later that day, Ira was standing at the front of a packed lecture hall, handing back a graded assignment. His course was so popular that students were sitting in the aisles.

"I've graded your first research papers," he told them, "and as you can see, there was a shocking statistical anomaly. Pretty much all of you got A's."

There was a delighted whoop from the class.

"Truth is," Ira went on, "I have a real good feeling about this group, and something tells me the parade of A's is going to continue right through the end of the semester. So much for those bell curves, right?"

There was a ripple of knowing laughter among the students, who knew all about bell curves. These were a method used by teachers who wanted to distribute grades evenly, giving out only a few A's, a few F's, and the rest somewhere in the middle. The whole class knew that Mr. Kane didn't care enough to bother with an annoying system like that. They were happy to share his cynicism.

"Bell curves suck, man!" a jock called out.

Two hands went up. One belonged to Deke Donald, the other to his brother Danny.

"Uh . . . Mr. Kane?" said Deke, holding up his paper. "Seems to be a mistake here. My brother and I each got a C minus on our papers."

"Yeah, me too," said Danny redundantly.

"Ah," said Ira, "the Donald twins."

"Actually, we're not twins, we're six months apart," said Danny. "Mom says that she and Dad made me on the day my brother was born."

Ira just looked at him. "Thanks for sharing," he said. "Now let me share something with you."

The Donalds looked at Ira eagerly.

"Last night," said Ira, "when I was grading papers, I came across two gems, both entitled 'Cells Are Bad.' Each paper had just one paragraph: 'Cells are bad. My uncle lives in a cell. It's ten feet by twelve. And he has to read the same old magazine every day. The end.'"

"That's just like our papers," Deke whispered loudly to Danny.

Ira rolled his eyes. "Please understand," he said, "though my standards may not be what they used to, I still could not bring myself to write the letter A on top of those beauties. Hope you understand."

"Sure," said Deke graciously.

"Hey, thanks, man," Danny chimed in.

Ira looked at them, shaking his head with dismay for the future of America.

— — —

Meanwhile, in the science building, Ira's friend Harry was on the phone in his cluttered office. The words HARRY BLOCK, ADJUNCT PROFESSOR OF GEOLOGY were stenciled on the door. Women's volleyball posters hung everywhere on the walls.

"In the desert?" he was saying into the phone. "Of course I'll go check it out. Meteors are my life."

Harry Block had always enjoyed life, perhaps a bit too much. He was a good-looking guy in his late twenties, a few years younger than his friend Ira. Teaching had never been Harry's highest priority.

Harry jotted something down as the person on the other end spoke. "Route seventeen. Got it. Rest assured, I will be there."

Harry hung up. Then he picked a blue exam book up from his desk and turned to the student who was sitting across from him, waiting patiently for his attention. Her name was Nadine.

Nadine was twenty. She was very, very cute, and she wore a tight pink half-shirt. "So," she said, "how's it look, Professor?"

Harry looked up at her. "It's tight," he said. He was talking about her grade, but he was focusing on her shirt.

"It's really, really tight—but not too tight, you know?"

Nadine smiled slyly.

"But you just don't have the points, Nadine," Harry said, recovering himself and looking back at the exam. "Sorry. Don't take it too hard, geology is a lot tougher subject than people think."

"Couldn't you check again?" Nadine asked in a kittenish voice. "I really need this credit to get into nursing school."

"Nursing school, huh?" Harry commented. "That's noble, but maybe you'd be more comfortable in a different profession. One where people's lives weren't dependent on you. Like phone sales. Or gymnastics."

"Actually, what I really want to be is Miss Arizona. But my pageant consultant told me that nursing school would really impress the judges. Makes you look like you wanna help people." She got up slowly and walked fetchingly over to Harry's side of the desk. "Bring joy to mankind," she murmured.

"Like Mother Teresa," said Harry, watching her move.

"Isn't there some kind of extra-credit assignment I could do . . . ?" Nadine offered, pushing his chair back and placing her hands on his shoulders.

"Well, uh, I guess you could write a research paper or something. How's that sound?"

Nadine looked crestfallen at the idea of doing actual work. "Can't I just—you know . . ." she suggested.

There was a knock at the door, cutting Nadine off midsentence and practically sending Harry flying off his chair.

The door opened and Ira stuck his head in. "Ready for lunch?" he asked. He stopped short when he saw Nadine standing in front of Harry.

"Just concluding a teacher-student conference here, Ira," said Harry.

"Uh-huh," said Ira. "Your dedication to your job is an inspiration to us all."

Harry looked at him, frustrated. Could Ira's timing get any worse? Then he turned back to Nadine. "Regrettably, Nadine," he told her, "I have a prior lunch engagement with Professor Kane." He took a deep breath. "Which means we'll have to discuss your extra-credit assignment at a later date."

■ ■ ■

In a little while, the two friends were traveling down the road in Harry's Jeep.

"Of course she left you," Harry was telling Ira. "You have no lust for life, no juice. . . ."

Ira shot him a look. "I have plenty of lust," he said, "and I'm full of juice."

"Women are always searching for a man with a passion for life," Harry lectured. "Someone like me. Maybe I can help you out, set you up with somebody. Does she have to be a witch like your last girlfriend?"

"She has to have her own shirts, that's for sure." Ira smiled wryly.

After few minutes, Ira looked around at the desert terrain

they were driving through. "Where are you taking me?" he asked Harry.

"Some meteor hit last night,"

"*That's* what that was," said Ira.

"Yup. And, as the official Glen Canyon representative of the U.S. Geological Survey, I've been assigned to go check it out. I need you to come with me in case I actually have to do something scientific. Then we'll eat."

Ira stared incredulously at Harry. "*You're* an official representative of the USGS?" he said.

Harry shrugged. "I signed up over the Internet." He grinned.

The Jeep made its way along a desert road, kicking up dust behind it. Finally, it came up over a ridge, and there in front of them was a large clearing in the desert near a big hole in the ground. Several police vehicles and other cars were parked nearby, and the area had been cordoned off with yellow police tape.

Harry stopped the Jeep, and he and Ira walked over to the clearing, where a group of policemen were trying to hold back the spectators who were trying to get a look into the hole.

Nearby, Wayne and some cops worked to rock Wayne's car and tip it back on its wheels. Wayne, covered in black soot, looked as if he'd been up all night. The sheriff, whose name was Jack Long, was watching the scene.

Wayne was all worked up. "I want to know who's gonna pay me for the damage to my car!" he yelled.

"I told you," the sheriff replied, "we don't do that. It's force majeure!"

"Force majeure, my ass!" said Wayne, not knowing or caring what the phrase meant. All he cared about was his car. "That car's a classic seventy-three Cutlass!"

Harry and Ira had now reached the scene. Harry was carrying a metal case.

"We'll take it from here, Cappy," Harry to the sheriff, trying to sound official.

Sheriff Long turned and looked Harry and Ira over. "Who the hell are you?" he said.

Harry pulled out his wallet and flashed his card as though it was a badge. "Harry Block, United States Geological Survey," he said. "This is my secretary, Ira Kane." Harry turned to Ira, gave him a "check me out" look, and then turned back to the sheriff. "We're here to . . . uh . . . investigate the meteor," he went on. "If indeed that's what it is."

Ira rolled his eyes.

Wayne looked at Harry. "Of course it's a meteor!" he shouted. "And it almost wrecked my car!"

"Calm down," the sheriff said to Wayne. "I'm still a little suspicious about what you were doing out here in the first place."

"For the thousandth time," said Wayne in infinite frustration. "I was practicing for my fireman's exam, which, for your information, started seven minutes ago. So I'd really appreciate it if you'd let me get out of here."

Ira was now looking around at the area, sizing it up. He turned his focus on Wayne. "You found the meteor?" he asked.

"Found?" Wayne repeated. He was talking slowly, as if to a child. "It bounced my car two hundred feet into the air."

"And you touched it?" Ira asked Wayne.

Harry turned to Ira. "Good question, Secretary Kane," he said. He turned to Wayne. "I hope you didn't touch the specimen," he said. "That's a major no-no from a geological standpoint."

"This is bull," said Wayne, fed up. "I didn't touch anything. Can I go?"

"He can go," Harry said to the sheriff. "Don't leave town," he told Wayne, in what he hoped was an authoritative-sounding voice.

Ira had turned his attention to the enormous hole in the ground. "Any other way into that cavern?" he asked Sheriff Long.

The sheriff pointed. "There's an old mine entrance just over that ridge," he said. "It'll lead you down there."

● ● ●

Soon Harry and Ira were working their way through the dark cave, which was illuminated only by the little lights on their USGS hard hats. Abruptly, they turned a corner in the cave and found themselves in a huge, open cavern. It must have been a good ninety feet high and three times as wide.

The space felt almost like a cathedral. The sunlight shin-

14

ing through the ten-foot hole at its top gave the cavern a soft, magical glow.

"I believe we've located the target," said Ira. He pointed to the large meteor in the corner of the cavern. It was fifteen feet tall, its point stuck into the ground like a javelin. The way the light hit it seemed to give it an eerie bluish glow.

Three cops were standing around the meteor, posing for pictures with it. Harry approached them. He could see from their badges that their names were Johnson, Thompson, and Drake. "At ease, gentlemen," he said. "The Feds have arrived."

The cops turned to Harry and Ira. "Who let you down here?" Johnson said.

"Let's not get combative here, Lieutenant," Harry replied. "The USGS and local law enforcement have a long history of cooperation."

Ira now stepped in, his tone totally polite. "We need to take a couple of scientific samples," he said to the officer. "If that's okay with you," he added.

"Sure," said Johnson, completely mollified by this. "Whatever. We got all the photos we need."

The cops backed off, and Ira and Harry approached the meteor. They noticed at once that the bluish hue wasn't just from the light above. There was also a phosphorescent film on the rock.

"The thing hit last night and it's already covered in this crap?" said Harry, amazed.

Ira crouched down for a closer look, a genuinely curious expression on his face. There was something very strange, even otherworldly, about this blue-green patina.

"What? What is it?" Harry asked him nervously.

Ira shrugged. "Nothing," he said, getting up. "It's probably just some kind of cave moss." He opened the metal case. "Let's get a couple of samples," he said.

He handed Harry a little pick from the case. "Here," he said. "Make the geological community proud."

Harry crouched down and began chipping away a section of the meteor.

Then Ira saw it: a clear, viscous liquid, seeping out of the meteor at the spot where Harry had chipped the piece off. The drops looked almost like tears.

"Jeez," said Harry, "it's like—like it's goozing."

"Goozing?" Ira echoed.

"Like gushing and oozing," said Harry.

"How very scientific of you," Ira said. "Put on some gloves."

CHAPTER THREE

The next day, Wayne's beat-up Cutlass rolled up in front of the fire station, and he emerged from the car laden with his yellow fire suit, an ax, and the charred dummy. The dummy's bottom half was burned completely off. He walked across the street to the firehouse driveway, where his friend Nick Simmons stood polishing a beautiful red hook-and-ladder truck.

"Oh man, you look awful," said Nick when he spotted Wayne. Then he noticed the dummy. "And what happened to Bernice?" he added.

"Don't ask," said Wayne glumly.

"How was the test?"

"The test was a piece of crap," said Wayne. "I only had ten minutes to take the written part, and then I hit the wall on the obstacle course. . . ."

Nick was sympathetic. "It's a long course," he said. "Lotta guys don't make it through."

"No," said Wayne, "I literally hit the wall. Ran right

into it, face first. Missed the rope completely."

Nick grimaced. "Ooh . . . that's bad," he said.

"Real bad. They won't even let me blow out a match in this town, let alone be a fireman," said Wayne. He walked into the firehouse and dropped his equipment inside.

"Well," said Nick, "at least you still got the pool gig over at the country club."

"I can't be slingin' towels my whole life."

"Listen, anytime you want to borrow any of this stuff to practice," Nick offered, "you just tell me. No one has to know."

"Thanks, man. I'm not givin' up on this." Wayne looked up at the gleaming fire truck with envy. Then he turned and started walking back to his car.

"Hey," Nick called after him, "I'm still cool to play the Mesa Verde course, right? 'Cause I finally got my driver working."

"Sure," Wayne replied sadly. "I can get you in anytime."

— — —

Over at the community college, Ira was at the table in the biology lab, carefully shaving off a part of the meteor specimen. Harry was sitting nearby, munching on a submarine sandwich.

"We have the match of the season against Arizona Tech," Harry was griping as he chewed, "and I'm stuck in a lab playing with rocks." He turned and looked at Ira. "Are you listening to me?" he asked.

Ira looked up from his work. "Don't talk with your mouth full—it's disgusting," he said.

Harry continued talking with his mouth full. "I'm starting to think this Geological Survey gig isn't all it's cracked up to be," he said. "I mean, yes, it pads out my resume, but is it making me grow as a person? As a Division Three women's volleyball coach?"

Focused on the specimens, Ira barely listened. He took a long metal tubelike instrument and used it to transfer some of the liquid that was seeping from the rock specimen into a series of test tubes.

"Are you going to do all those spectro-thingie tests that it says to do in the guidebook?" Harry wanted to know.

"Spectrograph," said Ira. "Yes, I will do a full spectroscopic analysis. Your resume will shine."

Ira's sarcasm was wasted on Harry. "Good. Lemme know if you find anything," he said cheerfully.

After Harry was gone, Ira kept working all afternoon and into the night. He squinted into the bright field of a four-hundred-power microscope, hardly believing what he was seeing. The sample on the slide was teeming with one-celled organisms that were very much alive. Each one had a nucleus. They were dividing at an astounding rate, multiplying furiously.

"This is incredible," Ira muttered to himself.

Before Ira's eyes, the cells multiplied so rapidly, in fact, that they quickly took over the entire area under the slide and cracked right through the glass slide cover.

Ira jumped involuntarily, startled at the activity under the microscope. He turned to the computer next to him and hit a few keys on the keyboard. In a moment, a screen came up, titled "NMR DNA Analysis." A screen full of data came up below the title.

"Ten base pairs," Ira mumbled, looking at the data generated by the nuclear magnetic resonance test. "That can't be. . . ." He hit the keys again, and the screen came up exactly the same. Ira just sat there staring at it, a look of disbelief spreading across his face.

● ● ●

In the gymnasium, the stands were full of cheering spectators. Tonight the Glen Canyon Desert Hens were taking on the Arizona Tech Roadrunners in a fierce women's volleyball match. Harry was on the sidelines, coaching his heart out.

"Dammit, Tina, you have to cover the line when Leona goes up for the spike!" he screamed at his team.

Ira walked into the gym and headed over to Harry on the sidelines. His excitement showed all over him.

A Tech player spiked the ball over the net. One of the women on Harry's team went up for the block, and the ball grazed off her hand and shot out of bounds. The whistle blew and the ref signaled a point for Arizona Tech.

"Two hands, Liza!" Harry yelled. "God gave you two hands for a reason!"

Ignoring all this, Ira approached Harry. He was totally pumped. "You might want to sit down for this, Harry," he said intensely. "The meteor samples are teeming with one-celled organisms. And their metabolic rates are off the charts. They're dividing at an incredible pace. Practically exponential."

Harry stared at Ira. "Do you have any idea how close this match is?" he said.

Then he refocused on the game. "Let's get the serve back! No mercy!" he shouted at his team.

Ira was insistent. "Harry," he said, "listen. I did an NMR and an electrospectrograph on the cells. Their DNA has ten base pairs."

"Ten base pairs?" Harry repeated without interest. "Yeah, great . . . *Tina!* Cover the line! *The line!*" he yelled angrily to the team.

"The DNA of all life on Earth," Ira continued, "only has four base pairs."

"So we're a few base pairs short," said Harry in irritation. "Will you let me work here?"

Ira grabbed Harry by the shoulders, turned him around, and looked him in the eye. "Harry," he said slowly and clearly. "These are one-celled organisms from another world. They're aliens."

They stared at each other for a long moment. Then Harry stood up. "Time out!" he shouted to the referee.

The ref blew the whistle, and Harry turned to Ira.

"Aliens . . . ? From outer space?" he said.

● ● ●

Having finally caught on, Harry accompanied Ira back to the lab. "Is the Nobel Prize paid in a lump sum or annual installments?" he asked Ira as they walked in the door.

"Look, let's not get ahead of ourselves here, okay?" said Ira.

"What do you think the taxes on that will be?"

"Just look in the microscope," said Ira.

They went over to the lab table and Harry stepped up to the microscope. "I'm all tingly," he said.

Now, as Ira looked on eagerly, Harry looked into the microscope. "Wow," Harry said. "Aliens." Then he looked up from the microscope and turned to Ira. "Uh . . . Ira," he said, "I'm no biologist, but how many cells do single-celled organisms have?"

"Please take this seriously, Harry. If we're going to be important scientists, we have to act the part." Ira bent down and looked into the eyepiece. "That can't be," he said.

But it was. Among the single-celled organisms on the slide, there were a few distinct many-celled creatures.

"There are multicellular organisms here!" said Ira, surprised.

"Yes," said Harry. "I know."

Ira scratched his head. "They weren't there before," he said.

"So they snuck in there somehow," said Harry.

"Impossible. It's been isolated and sealed the entire time. And it's from deep within the meteor."

"Well, how'd they get in there?"

Ira looked intently at Harry.

"What?" asked Harry, wondering why Ira was staring at him like that. "Do I have something on my teeth?"

"It's evolution, Harry," Ira told him slowly. "Right in front of our eyes. It's crazy, but it's possible. They're evolving. Two hundred million years' worth in just a few hours. . . ."

CHAPTER FOUR

Out in the desert the next day, two local cops, Johnson and Drake, were sitting on the hood of their squad car, shooting the breeze. They were guarding the roped-off area around the cavern where the meteor had crashed.

"You want to make detective," Sam Johnson was telling Drake, "you gotta be at the top of your game. The department's changed, it's a meritocracy these days."

Drake nodded, soaking in this advice.

"Used to be," Johnson went on, "you'd make detective like it was your birthright. But now, most of these new guys on the job are college boys. Guys like us gotta go the extra mile, we gotta be the better cops."

A faint sound could be heard in the distance. It was getting louder, like the sound of a vehicle approaching.

"You really know the ropes, man," Drake said. "I lucked out, being partnered with you."

"Watch me, listen to me, learn from me," Johnson said. "The work is everything."

They turned to see a school bus pulling up to the cave area. It was followed by a flatbed truck that was equipped with a hoist and winch. Out of the truck climbed the Donalds.

The school bus door opened and Ira stepped out, followed by Harry, Nadine the cute geology student, and a few other students. Nadine was wearing stylish open-toed sandals.

Harry noticed them, of course. "Nice footwear," he said to Nadine.

"I try," she replied sweetly.

"Perfect for spelunking," Ira added sarcastically. Then he turned to the group. "Now, class," he warned them, "remember: Don't touch anything, don't move anything, don't even breathe unless we tell you. And wear your protective gloves at all times."

The jock from Ira's class raised his hand. "Uh . . . Professors? What exactly are we doing here?"

"Firsthand field experience, that's what," said Harry. "The very meat and potatoes of geology. It's not all glamour, you know."

"Is this gonna be on the final?" Danny Donald wanted to know.

"Yes," Ira and Harry snapped at once.

Officer Johnson turned to Ira. "Hey, Professor, what's up?" he asked.

"Came to pick up the rock," said Ira as casually as possible.

"Uh-huh," said Johnson without a lot of interest.

"Yep," Harry added. "Orders from the U.S. Geological Survey. They want it under controlled conditions. It's technical."

"We'll just haul it out of here," said Ira.

Johnson thought this over. In the silence, Drake watched to see what Johnson would do.

"Sure," said Johnson finally. "Okay." He turned to Drake and grinned. "Looks like you and me are going home early today," he said.

Slowly, Ira and Harry led the students underground. There, just as they had left it, sat the meteor. It was bathed majestically in a shaft of light from the hole above.

There was a more ethereal look to the cave now. A foot-deep layer of misty gas hovered just above the ground around the meteor.

Harry eyed it suspiciously. "Is it me," he said to Ira, "or is this place getting a lot creepier?"

Ira turned to a student who was carrying a suitcase full of equipment. "Hand me the analyzer," he said.

The student had no idea what Ira was talking about, so Ira went to the suitcase himself and pulled out an instrument that tested the chemical composition of gases.

Nadine was holding her nose. "Harry, it smells disgusting in here," she complained.

"Science sometimes stinks. That's just the game we play, babe," he replied, playing the jaunty geologist. But then he turned to Ira and whispered, "Ira, this rotten egg thing is a real mood killer."

Ira, busy reading the analyzer, ignored him. "Hydrogen sulfide, methane, ammonia," he said to himself, studying the gauges and thinking hard. "It's like they're converting the atmosphere."

Harry pointed his flashlight at some strange growth that was springing out of the rock formations.

"Rudimentary plant life . . ." mused Ira.

Harry leaned over to him and whispered, pointing upward. "Are they . . . you know . . . alien?" he asked.

Ira subtly nodded in the affirmative. He didn't want to alarm the students.

They now stopped at the edge of the mist. Ira looked up at the opening. "Deke, Danny. Lower the winch!" he yelled.

Up above, the cops were waving their arms, directing the Donalds as they backed the flatbed toward the opening. When the truck was in position, the two boys jumped out of the truck. "Time to do science!" Danny yelled enthusiastically to his brother.

The cable was lowered carefully into the cave, where Ira, Harry, and a few of the students were waiting to grab the descending wire.

"I don't want to get all girly here," said Nadine, "but I feel something wiggling around my toes."

"Don't look at me," teased Harry. "My hands are right here."

The group continued to move forward, closer to the meteor.

"Well," Nadine persisted, "something's definitely playing with my feet."

Then, through the mist, Ira saw something. "Hold it!" he cried.

Everyone froze.

"Stop the winch, Danny!" Harry yelled up to the surface.

The cable stopped moving, and Ira, now joined by Harry and Nadine, crouched down and looked at the ground.

"What is it, chief?" Harry asked Ira.

Ira kept looking down. "The ground is . . . it's moving," he said.

"Oh my God, it's alive!" cried Harry. He pointed his flashlight down to where Nadine was standing. The mist swirled and eddied, revealing—

Eeeewww!

There were thousands and thousands of them, powder-blue flatworms with weird metallic casings. They crawled on Nadine's bare toes, all over the ground, on the bottom of the meteor, everywhere.

"Uchhhh! That's so disgusting!" cried Nadine.

"Yes, it is," said Harry. "Better let me hold you."

"Flatworms," said Ira thoughtfully, pulling on a pair of rubber gloves as he mulled over this new development. "Barely eighteen hours and we've got flatworms."

Using a pair of forceps, Ira picked up one of the flatworms and brought it out of the mist to have a better look at it. As soon as it was exposed to the air, however, it started writhing, then shriveling up.

"It's dying," said Harry.

28

"The oxygen's killing them," Ira said. He took a specimen jar, a glass one with a screw-on top, scooped up a few of the flatworms from the misty surface, and put them into the jar. Then he closed the jar, making sure it contained enough of the gaseous atmosphere for them to survive.

Standing up, he looked over at Harry, and then at the winch. "We better leave the meteor where it is," he said.

— — —

Later that afternoon, Ira and Harry were sitting at an outdoor table at the campus café. The jar with the flatworms was sitting on the table between them. Harry was finishing off a hamburger, while Ira's slice of pizza sat uneaten in front of him. Ira looked dazed, as if something large had hit him.

"It took us a billion years to do what they did in just a couple of days," he said.

"Yeah?" said Harry. "Those little germs are the embodiment of the American dream."

Along came Nadine. "Sorry to interrupt, Professor Block," she said to Harry, "but I was wondering if I'm right to assume that the field trip fulfills my missing credit requirements?"

"You know, Nadine," he said, "you're such a bright girl. If you would just focus. . . ."

Suddenly, Harry was not focusing. He was being distracted by something he noticed in the jar.

"Hey!" said Nadine. "One of the wormy things is breaking."

They were looking at a flatworm, gray, half an inch long. A small gap was beginning to open at the bottom of the creature.

"It's not breaking," Ira explained, "it's splitting. Mitosis. They reproduce by mitosis."

"Mitosis?" Harry joked for Nadine's benefit. "What, no sex?"

"No time for sex," said Ira grimly.

"Bummer," said Nadine.

Before their eyes, the flatworm split right in two. Two separate worms now wiggled side by side. One looked exactly like the original, but the other had mutated. It was darker and bigger.

Ira stared at the worms. "Look at the degree of mutation after only one generation."

"Yeah, I'm blown away," said Nadine, popping her gum. She turned to Harry. "So, what about it, Professor? Do I get the credit?" she asked him.

"Okay. Yes. Congratulations, you pass."

Nadine jumped up and down. "Great!" she squealed. "Thank you. I loved your course. You're a really good teacher."

She skipped away, and Harry turned to Ira. "She plans to be the next Miss Arizona," he informed his friend.

CHAPTER FIVE

That night, Ira and Harry went over to the biology lab to conduct some research. They worked deep into the night.

In the morning, they headed for the desert in Harry's Jeep.

"We call no one," said Ira as they sped down the road. "We tell no one. Not until we know exactly what we're looking at."

"Are you sure about that?" Harry asked. "Isn't this the kind of thing the government usually gets involved in? Maybe we should call them."

"Absolutely not. I know those people, Harry."

"You do?"

"This is our discovery," said Ira, "and we've got to ride it out. We need to do more research, make sure about our findings. We document everything. We take meticulous notes— keep control. All the time maintaining—"

"Absolute secrecy," said Harry, finishing Ira's thought.

Suddenly, a military helicopter came swooping overhead. Ira looked nervously over at Harry.

"Please tell me there's an air show today," said Harry.

They drove up over the last ridge—and there, sprawled out in front of them, was a world that hadn't been there the day before.

It was an enormous military installation. Military helicopters churned the air above the meteor's impact site, and there were more choppers on the ground. Trucks hustled in and out, delivering equipment. Over the cave itself, crews of soldiers were building a large research structure.

Harry and Ira watched the frenetic activity in horror.

"They found out," said Ira.

"How?" Harry asked, knowing that Ira didn't know the answer.

They kept driving, and Harry pulled up to a sentry station. Two military sergeants, each with an M-16 rifle, were standing guard at the entrance to the newly created compound. Their names were Toms and Larson.

"Can I help you?" Sergeant Toms asked them.

Harry tried his official thing. "Harry Block and Ira Kane. U.S. Geological Survey," he said.

Sergeant Toms inspected his clipboard.

"We're conducting some important research," Ira told him. "This is our site."

"Not anymore," Sergeant Toms informed him. "I'm sorry, you're not on the list."

"What do you mean, we're not on the list?" said Harry. "We come here all the time."

Toms was not amused. "This isn't a nightclub, pal. Take it somewhere else."

"Hey, I know my constitutional rights!" Harry protested. "You can't—"

Ira put up his hand and stopped Harry. Arguing with these guys was useless. "Look," he said to Sergeant Toms, "could you please call your superior and tell him that we'd like to have a word with him?"

Toms took a step back and picked up his walkie-talkie. "I've got a Harry Block and an Ira Kane out here," he said into it. "Claim they have some kind of connection to the site. . . ."

Sergeant Larson had now pricked up his ears. He turned to Ira. "Did you say Kane?" he asked him.

Ira nodded.

"Ira Kane . . . ? *The* Ira Kane?" Suddenly, Larson got a steely look in his eyes. "You bastard!" he shouted at Ira, lifting his machine gun and pointing it directly at Ira.

Sergeant Toms, still occupied with the walkie-talkie, had not yet noticed this. "Yes, sir. . . . Right away, sir," he was saying into the mouthpiece. Then he saw Larson. "What the hell are you doing?" he yelled.

Toms jumped in front of Larson and wrestled his gun away from him.

"You don't know what it was like!" Sergeant Larson bawled. He turned to Ira, furious. "You're responsible for the worst month of my life!" he shouted.

Sergeant Toms had all he could do to restrain Larson. "Go!" Toms yelled at Harry. "Drive! Straight ahead—someone will meet you!"

Harry floored it, driving into the compound. "What was *that* about?" he said to Ira.

Ira did not reply.

Inside, Harry and Ira got out of the Jeep and headed toward the briefing tent. All around them, the place was alive with construction activity. A large plastic tarp was being secured over the hole where the meteor had punched into the cave.

The tent flap opened, and a lieutenant emerged to usher Harry and Ira inside. He introduced himself as Lieutenant Cryer. He looked like a decent guy.

At a table inside the tent stood a military big shot, going over some papers with his aide. Just as it was clear that Lieutenant Cryer was a nice guy, something in the manner of these two immediately conveyed the feeling that they were not men to be trusted.

Ira knew them. The big shot was Dr. Russell Woodman, the highest ranking scientist in the army. The aide was named Colonel Flemming.

"What are you doing here, Russell?" Ira said to Woodman.

"Ira . . . what an unexpected surprise," said Woodman, not looking surprised at all. He walked over and embraced Ira. There was an uncomfortable look on Ira's face.

"Yeah, for me, too," Ira replied. "I didn't realize we were on a hugging basis."

Woodman laughed a hearty laugh. "The same old Ira Kane," he said. He turned to Harry. "And you must be . . ." he said.

Ira made the introductions. "Harry Block, this is General Russell Woodman, the head of U.S. Army Research."

"You guys know each other?" Harry said to Ira in surprise.

"Ira used to work with me," said Woodman. "Right, Ira?"

Now Harry was even more surprised. "You were a big shot in army research? In the Pentagon?" he said, not noticing how uncomfortable Ira looked. "No kidding. I thought you were in the shmatah business."

Ira turned to Woodman. "How did you find out about this?" he said.

Woodman smiled. "You leave the Pentagon, you don't call, you don't write . . . We like to keep tabs on our prodigal sons."

"So, what . . . you tapped my phone?" said Ira.

"We're not the KGB, Ira," chuckled Woodman. He threw a glance toward Flemming.

"Actually," said Flemming, "we've been monitoring your computer."

Suddenly Harry was nervous. "His computer?" he said. "The girls in those photos are all *over* eighteen!"

"I should've figured," Ira said to Woodman in disgust.

"Yes, you should've," Woodman returned. "And you should've known better than to keep something this big from us."

"And the Centers for Disease Control," said a woman's voice.

Harry and Ira spun around to see an attractive and intelligent-looking woman enter the tent.

"Good, just in time," Woodman said to her. "Ira, this is Dr. Allison Reed, senior researcher in epidemiology at the CDC."

Allison extended her hand. "Dr. Kane. Your reputation precedes you," she said. But as she stepped forward, her foot got caught on the leg of a chair, causing her to flop over and land headfirst at Ira's feet, revealing an unexpected flash of very nice underwear.

Ira tried not to smile as he and Woodman moved to help her up. But she pushed them away as she stood and straightened out her clothing. "It's okay. Thank you. I can do this myself," she said, in a way that indicated that she was used to collecting herself off the floor.

Finally, she launched into the speech she'd been planning to give. "Dr. Kane," she said severely, "I had heard about your recklessness. But you were way out of line on this one. Do you realize how dangerous this situation could have become?"

"No need to play the blame game here, Dr. Reed," said Woodman. "No harm, no foul. Suffice it to say that we're all very appreciative of the discovery made by Dr. Kane and Mr. Block." He turned to Ira and Harry. "The confirmation of the existence of life outside our planet is—"

"One of the greatest scientific discoveries of our time," Ira finished.

There was a long, frozen beat. "Well . . . yes," agreed Woodman. "And you have my word that we'll keep you in the loop from this point forward."

"Keep us in the loop?" said Harry, not quite getting it.

Ira, however, knew just where this was heading. "You bastard," he said to Woodman.

Harry really got it now. He pointed to himself and Ira. "*This* is the loop!" he hollered.

Allison looked pained. "Yes, but—" she began.

Woodman cut her off. "We're just following protocol here, Ira. You remember protocol? Though, as I recall, you did have a little trouble with the concept back at the Pentagon."

"But it certainly was *your* specialty," Ira snapped.

Harry just looked on, totally confused.

"Look," said Allison, "this isn't a contest. The simple fact is that this research must continue under careful government control and scrutiny."

Flemming jumped in now. "We've already secured the area," he reported. "We're constructing an air lock into the cavern and a state-of-the-art field research facility."

"So, you see," Woodman said to Ira and Harry, "there

doesn't seem to be much left for the science department of Glen Canyon Community College to do."

Harry was hopping mad. "Did you hear that?" he said to Ira. "Did you hear the condescending way he said Glen Canyon Community College?"

Allison was trying to be reasonable. "We're following well-established federal guidelines," she said, "that mandate—"

Ira cut her off. "I knew you'd pull this crap," he said to Woodman. "We deserve to be here."

But Woodman was not moved by this. In fact, he was disquietingly calm. "Oh, you deserve to be here?" he replied. "You're lucky anyone's let you near a science lab again. You're a disgrace. And a dangerous one at that." With that, he motioned to Lieutenant Cryer. "Lieutenant, show these men out," he said brusquely.

CHAPTER SIX

Two weeks later, the front steps of the Glen Canyon Municipal Court Building were crowded with reporters, TV cameramen, and spectators. As police officers struggled to hold back the press, Woodman, Allison, and a team of government lawyers pushed through the crowds and into the building. They were carrying boxes of evidence and files.

The reporters barked questions at them. "Why all the secrecy?" asked one, shoving a microphone into their faces.

"Stand back!" yelled an officer. "This is a closed session!"

Woodman and Allison finally made their way through the gauntlet and stepped inside.

In the closed courtroom, Judge Joseph Guilder was presiding at the bench. Ira and Harry were at the plaintiffs' table. Allison, Woodman, his hard-nosed aide Colonel Flemming, and a team of government lawyers took their places at the defendants' table.

Judge Guilder began the questioning. "Dr. Kane," he

said, "are you asking me to bar the federal government from involvement in a discovery as substantial as this one?"

"We're asking you," Ira replied, "to insure that the local scientists who actually made the discovery continue to play a significant role."

"They've already kept us out for almost two weeks," Harry added. "We put our lives on the line to find these little guys, Your Grace, and we just want to be there for them as they grow up."

"We were the first team at the meteor site, and all the testing was done in our lab, Judge," Ira argued.

Woodman snorted. "The bio lab at Glen Canyon Community College? It's a joke."

Judge Guilder glared at Woodman. "It wasn't a joke when I went there, General," he said.

Suddenly, Woodman looked a little nervous. Ira smiled. The government lawyer glowered at Woodman. *Way to offend the judge,* his look said. *Nice going.*

Allison now rose. "Your Honor," she said, "if the court would allow me to depose Dr. Kane. . . ."

"That would be highly unusual," said the judge.

"Yes, Your Honor, but there's something we feel you should know about Dr. Kane's past. It may be helpful in your ruling."

Ira suddenly looked nervous. "My past?" he said. "How is that relevant?"

Woodman spoke to the judge, but he was looking straight

at Ira. "It goes to the issue of Dr. Kane's competence as a scientist," he said.

And so, Ira took the witness stand. He looked extremely uncomfortable. Allison approached him, carrying a fat folder.

"Dr. Kane," she began, "you were a top-level researcher at USAMRID from ninety-four to ninety-seven, were you not?"

"Yes, the Army Medical Research Division, that's correct."

"And you were summarily dismissed in the summer of nineteen ninety-seven. Any idea why?"

As Allison waited for his answer, she nervously began to fidget with the top button of her blouse.

"My services were no longer required," said Ira.

"Uh-huh," said Allison. "So in your opinion, your firing had nothing to do with an experimental anthrax vaccine that you developed and administered to nearly one hundred and forty thousand U.S. soldiers in May of that year?" She continued fiddling with her button as she spoke.

"I see where you're going," Ira said sourly. "It may have been a factor. You'd have to ask the Joint Chiefs about that."

This was the first time Harry had heard any of this, and it made him nervous.

"I'll make a note to do that," said Allison. "But for now, can you tell us what happened to the soldiers who were inoculated with your vaccine?"

"None of them got anthrax, if that's what you're asking," Ira said.

"What did they get?"

Ira was looking more and more uncomfortable. "It's not unusual for there to be certain side effects associated with a new vaccine," he said.

"Such as?" said Allison.

"Some gastrointestinal discomfort."

"Could you be more specific?" As Allison stepped closer to press her case, the button with which she had been absent-mindedly playing popped completely off.

"Well, there was a wide range of things," answered Ira, trying to stay focused.

Allison bent down and searched around on the floor for the button.

"It's so technical," Ira continued, "I'd hate to take the court's time."

"Humor us," said Allison from the floor.

Ira was very distracted and uncomfortable at this point. "Well, let's see," he said. "Severe diarrhea, anal—uh—leak-age . . . debilitating stomach cramps . . ."

"Go on," urged Allison, still groping around on the floor.

The judge looked down at her. "Everything okay there, Dr. Reed?" he asked.

Allison stood up. Without its missing button, her blouse was so low cut that it looked as if it belonged in a dance club instead of a courtroom.

"Yes, Your Honor, just fine," said Allison uncomfortably.

Suddenly realizing that her lacy bra was showing, she pulled her blouse shut with her hand.

She turned back to Ira, trying to regain her composure. "Uh . . . that's quite a list," she said. "Anything else?"

"I can't recall," said Ira. "It was a long time ago."

"Try," said Allison. She grappled with her file, which allowed her blouse to slip open again. Like a magnet, Ira's eyes were drawn right to her chest.

"Your Honor," said Allison in frustration, "could you please instruct the witness to stop staring down my blouse?"

"Hey, she's the one trying to distract me."

"I lost a button, let's not make a federal case out of it," said Allison.

The judge spoke up. "Just answer the question, Dr. Kane," he directed. "What were the other symptoms?

"Partial facial paralysis, memory loss, drooling, temporary blindness . . ." said Ira. "Uncontrollable flatulence."

As Harry incredulously watched Ira recite the symptoms, Woodman whispered something to Allison.

Allison stepped over to the witness box. "I think we get the idea," she said to Ira. "Do you happen to remember what the soldiers called this illness, Dr. Kane?"

Ira hesitated.

"Dr. Kane . . . ?" Allison prompted.

"They called it the Kane Madness," said Ira miserably.

And that was that. In very short order, the lawsuit came to

an end. Judge Guilder issued his opinion from the bench.

"In light of these revelations about Dr. Kane's reckless behavior," he said, "and considering the importance of this discovery, this court finds no basis for the plaintiffs' petition. I'm also granting the government's request for a gag order. Any public mention of these proceedings or the original discovery will be treated as contempt of this court and will be vigorously prosecuted. The plaintiffs' motion is denied."

As the judge slammed his gavel down, Woodman smiled a satisfied smile.

Harry and Ira walked out of the courtroom, totally deflated.

CHAPTER SEVEN

The Mesa Verde Country Club was Glen Canyon's oldest and most prestigious golf club. Around its palatial pool, the wealthy clientele lounged in chairs, being served drinks by pool boys.

Wayne, now wearing his country-club uniform and a disgruntled scowl, walked with a toolbox toward the pool's filtration system.

Before he got there, he was accosted by Barry Cartwright, a sixtyish golfer with an attitude.

"Hey, Wayne," said Cartwright.

Wayne stopped, dreading what was to come.

Cartwright held up a towel as if it were a dead skunk. "What's this?" he demanded to know.

"It's a towel, sir," said Wayne.

"What kind of towel?"

Wayne inspected it. "That would be an all-cotton towel, sir. I believe it's a Fieldcrest."

"It's a damp towel, Wayne," said Cartwright. "What the hell is a damp towel doing on my chaise?"

"It's drying out, sir?" Wayne guessed.

"Don't be a smarty," Cartwright said nastily. "The whole chaise is damp now."

"I'm sorry, sir. I'll get you a new one."

Cartwright could not just leave it alone. "You're pool manager, right?" he said snidely. "If there's anyone who'd know what to do about the dampness on my chair, it's you."

"I'm on it," Wayne said.

Cartwright nodded and walked off.

"Better hope there's never a fire at your house, jerk," Wayne muttered after he was out of earshot.

He picked up the wet towels, headed to the filtration room, and dumped them into a large laundry cart. But near the water-pump mechanism, something caught Wayne's eye. What the heck was that?

He looked more closely and saw hundreds of dead flat-worms, all shriveled up on the concrete. "It's a damn infestation," Wayne said aloud.

And what was that smell? "Whoa . . . it stinks in here," he added.

Now Wayne noticed something long and snakelike, swimming in the murky waters of the glass filtration tank. "What the hell . . . ?" he mumbled, bending closer to get a better look.

Wham! Something slammed into the glass right in front of Wayne—a nauseating, pink leechlike creature with a horrendous, sucking mouth! He fell back, startled.

— — —

After the court session was over, Harry and Ira walked dejectedly back to the biology lab.

"Damn!" Ira said. "She cut out my heart—and ate it!"

"Hey, you win some, you lose some," said the philosophical Harry. "Karma."

Ira just gave him look.

Harry grinned. "She likes you, you know," he said.

"What? Were you even in that courtroom?"

Harry was not deterred. "Trust me," he said. "Being mercilessly grilled like a common criminal, it's all teasing."

"Well, call me old-fashioned," said Ira, "but I prefer a more straightforward approach."

"At least," said Harry as they reached the door of the lab, "we still get credit for the discovery and the initial research. They can't take that away from us."

Or so they thought. Harry and Ira stepped into the lab to find that it had been totally taken apart, stripped clean. Files were strewn on the floor, there was broken glass everywhere, and nearly every test tube and specimen holder had been removed.

Ira just stared at the wreckage. "They've cleaned us out," he said finally.

"Those bastards!" cried Harry. "How can they do that? It's against the law!"

Ira rushed over to his computer and hit a few keys. "Damn," he muttered. "It's gone. All our data, the DNA sequencing, the J-PEG files—"

"My sandwich!" said Harry, who was looking into the fridge. "Those bastards took the other half of my sandwich!"

"We can't let them get away with this," Ira vowed.

"I'm calling the cops," said Harry.

"The cops?" Ira spluttered. "They *are* the cops!"

"Then, what?" said Harry.

● ― ●

That night Ira and Harry launched their counteroffensive. Dressed in military uniforms, they crouched behind a mound of dirt, looking down on the chain-link fence that surrounded the desert compound. Through a pair of binoculars, Ira watched as Woodman drove out through the gates.

Ira lowered his binocs. "He's out," he whispered to Harry. "Time to roll."

Silently, they edged up to the fence, where Harry cut the chain-link with a pair of wire cutters. He pulled open the hole, and they squeezed through.

They made their way cautiously toward the large geodesic dome that now covered the cavern.

As he walked beside Ira, Harry noticed the ranks displayed on their uniforms. "Hey, how come you get to be a colonel and I'm just a private?" he said.

"I was a colonel," Ira replied.

"Uh-huh. And you obviously served your country with distinction," Harry cracked.

"Just consider yourself lucky. The penalty for impersonating an officer is five years in military prison.

"Maybe for you," said Harry. "Me, they'd hang."

They were now approaching the entrance to the dome. Two MPs were standing guard outside it, having a smoke.

"Just act like you belong," Ira said quietly to Harry.

As they walked past the MPs, Ira glanced at the cigarette butt one of them had just dropped. "Pick that up, soldier," he said offhandedly.

Without even blinking, the soldier saluted Ira and then picked up the butt.

"Sorry, sir," he said as Ira and Harry walked right through.

Harry liked this. "And tuck in that shirt!" he barked at the soldier as he passed.

Inside the dome was a fully functional, state-of-the-art field research facility. Ira and Harry gaped in amazement at the complex setup. A thick plastic tarp, surrounded by tanks of compressed oxygen, covered the hole at the top of the cavern. There was a control room, a medical tent, and a specimen holding area.

"They've really done a lot with the place," murmured Ira.

The area was a hive of activity. The night crew of researchers and soldiers were going about their business, hustling to and fro.

Harry spotted Allison, who was crossing from the research tent into the control room. "Ice Queen at nine o'clock," he whispered, ducking behind a post.

Ira scooted behind the post to join Harry. Then he

stuck his head out, watching her as she walked.

True to form, she stumbled on something, accidentally dropping the enormous pile of research papers she was carrying.

"The lady's a menace," whispered Ira as they watched her bending down to recover the papers.

Harry just grinned.

Their attention was caught by two researchers who emerged from the staging area, wearing bio-containment suits. They passed in front of Harry and Ira's hiding place, carrying a clear plastic specimen case. In the case was a weird assortment of alien creatures.

Harry and Ira just stared.

In ten minutes, they had sneaked into the staging area and began donning bio-containment suits themselves. The suits were equipped with full oxygen packs and two-way radios.

"I feel like a jerk in this outfit," griped Harry.

"There's enough hydrogen sulfide, ammonia, and methane down there to kill us off in less than two minutes," Ira told him. "The suit's a good idea."

"But I look like a Solid Gold dancer," said Harry, looking down at himself.

They put their helmets on, now communicating through the two-way radios.

"Testing . . . testing . . . testing, one, two, three," said Harry.

Ira winced. "I hear you! Stop it!" he yelled inside his helmet. Then he grabbed an empty specimen case and they headed into the elevator.

Up in the control room, Lieutenant Cryer was surrounded by video monitors that were hooked up to the cameras scanning the cave. When he heard the elevator start up, he checked the monitors and saw two men in bio-containment suits stepping out of the elevator and into the air lock.

Cryer turned to Carla, his research assistant. "Who's that?" he asked her. He checked his clipboard. "I don't have anything on my schedule."

"Probably doing a nocturnal specimen run," she replied. "You know how those guys in sector twelve are."

"Yeah . . ." said Cryer uncertainly.

In the air lock, Ira and Harry moved through the antiseptic space toward the second door.

"Ready?" said Ira. He threw open the safety seal and the door whooshed open.

Suddenly, they were in an alien world. Weird plant life was everywhere—but the dominant color was a deep shade of blue, not green. Oddly shaped and textured vegetation now blanketed the rocks. Purple vines were crawling up the sides of the cave and had already spread to within a few feet of the top. A haze of poisonous mist hovered everywhere. It was as if Harry and Ira had traveled a mile under the ocean, except that there was no water.

And the critters! Hundreds of alien insects buzzed and flitted through the air. There were large ones, small ones, some having odd-looking metal casings. Others crawled across the ground.

Harry and Ira just stood there, taking it all in. "Do you believe this?" said Harry in wonderment. "Our little babies have grown up."

"I'm bursting with pride," Ira said.

Harry's gaze fell on a small tree. It had blue leaves and its trunk was covered in metallic-looking scales that looked rather like fish scales. The limbs were eerily menacing.

"Three weeks," said Harry, "and it's like a rain forest in here."

"Without the charm of the tropics," said Ira.

An animal suddenly stepped out from some bushes, wobbling on ten long, spindly legs. Harry and Ira stopped to watch it. Its body, two feet off the ground, was cylindrical, like a log. Six-inch spikes ran the length of its back. It had no obvious head or tail end. There was a circular mouth-thing on what might have been its underbelly. The whole effect was of a sort of bizarre, extraterrestrial walking log.

"Is it coming or going?" said Harry.

Ira was eyeing a long curtain of wet, pearl-like beads hanging down from the limb of an alien tree. It looked a bit like Spanish moss. The curtain swayed slightly.

The spindly log creature started to trot away, and as it did so, it brushed the hanging curtain. In a flash, the tendril-like tentacles sprang to life. They grabbed the helpless animal and wrapped themselves around it, lifting the struggling creature off the ground. It made small bleating sounds.

As Harry and Ira looked on with a mixture of revulsion and fascination, the creature was carried into the upper branches of the "tree." In seconds, the tentacles had swallowed the log creature completely. The struggle was over. It had been vicious, violent, and final.

"Damn," said Harry after a silence. "That tree just ate it."

Ira looked around. "Everything in here," he said, "is food for something else. Let's try not to be a part of the buffet."

They moved forward carefully. But soon, Harry took a step and heard a crunching sound. "Whoops," he said. He lifted his boot slowly to reveal a squished alien beetle. The crablike creature's hard shell had been crushed by Harry's boot.

Suddenly, three more of the crablike things appeared out of nowhere. They began feasting on the crushed beetle, their small multiple legs pumping furiously as they digested their dead compatriot.

"Yummy," said Harry.

Ira bent down to look. "Snag one while they're distracted," he said.

Reaching down with his specimen case, Harry tried to grab one of the creatures. It hissed loudly at him. He quickly withdrew his hand.

Harry was determined, though. "C'mon, you little bastards," he coaxed, chasing them around the cave. "I'm not going to hurt you."

He was so intent on his crab catching that he nearly ran into a much larger creature. It had long, muscular limbs and a curious double-humped body that looked remarkably like a human butt.

"Careful," Ira warned him.

As they watched, the butt-thing snatched one of the scurrying crabs and popped it into its mouth, crunching it up in no time.

"Now, who does that remind you of?" Harry said to Ira.

"What? What are you talking about?"

"C'mon," said Harry. "Take a close look. This isn't hard. She's been throwing it your way enough."

"Who?" Ira said, mystified.

CHAPTER EIGHT

A llison was at this moment not far away, sitting in a
meeting room with Flemming and going over some
reports. She looked up when Cryer entered the room.

"Did you authorize a walk-through?" Cryer asked her.

"Nope. Why?" she asked.

Cryer pointed to one of the monitors. There were Ira and
Harry, their backs to the camera, still checking out the butt-
headed alien.

Allison looked at them curiously. Then she turned up the
volume on the communication system so they could now hear
Ira and Harry's conversation.

"You mean Dr. Reed?" Ira was saying, blissfully unaware
that a roomful of people was now listening.

Flemming and Cryer looked furtively over at Allison.

"Bingo," said Harry, pointing to the creature. "See how
softly the curves on top come together."

"Yes—the image is very clear," said Ira.

"Now," said Harry, "picture Dr. Reed at a lab table, leaning over a Bunsen burner. . . ."

"I admire your assumption that there's actually a sexual human being underneath Reed's deep-seated neuroses," said Ira. "Personally, I don't buy it. She's a humorless geek."

This got a raised eyebrow from Allison, as Flemming and Cryer tried to suppress their laughter.

"That part's just a cover," Harry said. "Nothing some good loving won't cure."

"You think?" said Ira.

But Allison didn't want to know what Harry thought. She had heard enough. She whirled on Flemming and Cryer. "Suit up!" she ordered.

- - -

Down in the cave, Ira and Harry were in the process of chipping off a sample of the meteor. "C'mon," said Ira, "bag that and let's get the hell out of here."

A small dragonfly-like creature was buzzing around Harry's helmet.

"Ready whenever you are, Colonel," Harry responded. "This suit's making me chafe." He swatted at the fly. "Get away," he told it.

Suddenly he and Ira heard Allison's voice over the radios in their helmets. "Hold it right there," she said.

They turned to find Allison, Cryer, and Flemming standing behind them in bio-containment suits. Cryer and Flemming were carrying guns that were pointed straight at them.

"Busted," muttered Harry.

"Nice seeing you again," Ira said to Allison.

Allison was in no mood. "You do realize," she said, "you're in direct violation of the judge's orders. I could have you arrested right now."

"You're talking to me about violations?" Ira rejoined. "What about our lab?"

Flemming now had a nervous look on his face.

Meanwhile, Harry was bobbing and weaving, trying to avoid the pesky fly. The thing had a needlelike nose that was as long as its body. "Anybody got a can of Raid?" he said.

Allison ignored Harry, instead looking at Ira as if he was crazy. "What are you talking about?" she asked him.

"You stole our files," Ira said, "our samples, our computer hard drive . . ."

"Half of my sandwich!" Harry added, swatting at the bug. "Shoo, fly!" he yelled at it.

"I didn't steal anything," Allison said to Ira.

"Well, your friends cleaned us out," Ira replied.

Allison looked at Flemming suspiciously. Then she turned back to Ira. "I had no idea," she said.

Flemming, quite interested in changing the subject, didn't give her a chance to say any more. "The point is, this area is under military control and you're trespassing," he snarled at Ira.

During this whole exchange, Harry was still swatting at the bug, but the bug was not going away. It just kept hovering near him.

"Colonel," Allison said to Flemming, "I'll handle this."

"Hey, this thing won't leave me alone," Harry broke in.

"Harry, forget the bug," said Ira. "We're in a situation here."

"Right."

Harry took one final swat, and the thing seemed to disappear.

"Let's be honest here," Ira said to Allison and Flemming. "You've been trying to grab credit on our discovery from the start. All we're doing is taking back what's rightfully ours."

At this moment, where no one could see it, the dragonfly creature was perched on the back of Harry's neck.

"Credit has nothing to do with it," Allison told Ira heatedly. "I'm concerned about public safety!" She turned to confront Flemming. "Is this true?" she demanded. "Are you aware of any of this, Flemming?"

"No. Absolutely not," Flemming coolly lied. "None of it's true."

"And you believe him?" said Ira. "He openly admitted to monitoring my computer!"

On the back of Harry's suit, a metallic spike was now extending from the mouth of the dragonfly. In a swift downward motion, it thrust down and opened a small gash in the suit, just wide enough for the creature to slip inside.

Harry felt something on his back. "There's something in here," he said, twitching his shoulder.

Ira turned to look at him.

The meteor
that started it all.

Professor Harry Block and his "secretary,"
Dr. Ira Kane, arrive on the scene.

Ira and Harry take a sample
from the meteor.

Ira runs the sample through
a gauntlet of tests.

"It's like they're converting the atmosphere."

Lunch . . . and a new life-form.

Dr. Allison Reed clumsily interrogates her witness.

Kane prepares to infiltrate the government compound.

"I feel like a jerk in this outfit."

"MOMMY!!!!"

Glen Canyon Community College's finest check out the crash site.

In the Valley of the Dead Alien Birds.

Going after the alien,
the old-fashioned way.

Wayne
serenades
the alien bird.

U. S. Army General Russell Woodman—
doused and defeated.

Ira and Allison celebrate their success.

Harry was shouting now. "There's something in my suit!" he screamed.

Allison rolled her eyes.

"What?" Ira said to Harry.

"*Ahhhhh!*" shrieked Harry, starting to dance around as if he were at a disco. He jumped up and down, and began running around in circles, twirling like a maniac. "That bug is in my suit! Get it out! Get it out!"

"Turn up your oxygen mix!" Ira yelled.

Harry groped for the oxygen valve and started turning it. But in the meantime, the outline of the fly was moving around near Harry's butt.

"Sweet sister of God!" yelled Harry.

"Just relax, Harry," Ira said, "the oxygen's gonna kill it! Unless . . ."

Suddenly, the bulge in Harry's suit disappeared.

"Unless what?" Harry hollered.

Harry stopped moving for a second. There was momentary silence. And then . . .

"*Ahhhhhhhhhh! It's in me!*" Harry screamed.

● ● ●

Minutes later, a hospital gurney with Harry on it went slamming through two swinging doors that led to the medical unit of the research facility.

"*Ahhhhhhhhhh!*" he was still screaming.

His suit had been removed, and he was now dressed only in a T-shirt and briefs. The outline of the bug was clearly visible just under his skin. It was moving down his thigh now.

A squadron of doctors and nurses surrounded him, and soon he was being raced toward a procedure room, writhing around on the gurney. Ira and Allison were at his side.

"For the love of everything good and holy in this world, get this damn thing out of my body!" he howled.

"You're gonna be okay," Ira reassured him, not sounding terribly certain of the truth of this statement. He turned to the doctors. "Cut him open! Let's get this thing," he yelled.

On the gurney, Harry looked at Ira in horror. "Cut me *open*? There goes your stupid Christmas gift, Judas!"

The gurney was wheeled into the procedure area, the nurses all scurrying around Dr. Paulson, who was the surgeon in charge.

The bug was now moving down Harry's leg.

"It's moving down his leg!" Dr. Paulson diagnosed astutely.

"What do we do?" Allison asked worriedly.

"We might have to amputate!" said Dr. Paulson.

Harry's eyes popped out of their sockets. "Amputate? Are you out of your *minds*?" He grabbed Ira's hand. "Don't let them take my leg, man!" he begged.

Ira looked at the doctor. "Isn't there any other way?" he said. "He thinks he's an athlete."

The bug had changed direction. It was now headed *up* his leg, toward . . .

"It's headed for his privates!" said the doctor.

Harry's face turned white. "Amputate!" he yowled. "Take my leg! Please!"

But the bug was still on the move. It hung a sharp left, toward Harry's other leg.

"No!" gasped Allison. "It's going to the other side!"

Dr. Paulson didn't waste a second. "Get me some forceps!" he ordered. "I might be able to catch it in his colon!"

"How are you going in?" Allison asked him.

"Rectally!"

"*Mommy!!!!!*" Harry wailed loudly.

The nurse thrust a pair of forceps into the doctor's hands. "Lubricant?" she asked him.

"There's no time!" said the doctor.

"What?!" Harry cried indignantly. "There's always time for lubricant!"

"Flip him!" ordered the doctor.

They turned Harry's body over, and the doctor grasped the forceps.

"Here we go," said the nurse.

"Sweet mother in heaven!" prayed Harry.

Ira gripped Harry's hand hard. "Just relax, Harry," he said.

"*Relax?* Here, let me stick this gurney up your butt, see how you relax!"

Harry moaned and clenched his teeth as the doctor felt around with the forceps. "A little more," the doctor said, working the forceps. "a little deeper . . ."

"No more! No deeper!" yelled Harry.

And then the doctor pulled the forceps out—

"Sweet sister of Christ!" Harry said.

—with the dragonfly gripped in its pincers. "Got it!" the doctor announced.

"Don't you ever do that again!" Harry yelled at the doctor.

The doctor held the creature up with the forceps. It writhed around, choking from the oxygen. Then it died.

Ira bent over to soothe the extremely agitated Harry. "It's dead, Harry, it's dead," he told him.

"The oxygen killed it," Allison said.

"Was it a *painful* death?" Harry whimpered hopefully.

Allison and Ira watched as the doctor dropped the small carcass into a metal tray. "It looked pretty bad, yeah," Ira replied.

"Good. Can I have ice cream?" Harry asked.

"Sure," said Allison. "What flavor?"

"Doesn't matter," Harry answered.

"It's for his butt," Ira explained.

He and Allison exchanged a smile.

CHAPTER NINE

I t was the night of the Mesa Verde Country Club's seventh annual Charity Luau. The decadence of the rich was on display in all its tasteless glory. Two hundred Glen Canyon socialites, dressed in Hawaiian shirts, hula skirts, and adorned in leis were doing the limbo, gobbling down barbecue, and generally making fools of themselves.

Behind the bar, Wayne and the rest of the pool boys were dressed like Hawaiian warriors. Wayne was the head bartender for the night.

Wayne was just about at the end of his tether. "I'm a Hawaiian warrior," he muttered to his young assistant, Tommy. "*Yeesh.* Y'know, I'm thinking seriously about moving. Maybe down to California. Start over."

"Because of the fireman thing?" responded the extremely laid-back and hygienically challenged Tommy. "Big deal, you flunked out. You know how many times I've flunked in my life? A *ton.* And look at me!"

Looking at Tommy was not going to make Wayne feel a lot better.

Up to the bar sauntered the ever-obnoxious Barry Cartwright. "Hey, pool boy," he said to Wayne in an ugly tone, "you watering down the Mai Tais?"

Wayne was in the middle of mixing a drink. "No, sir," he said. "But let me fix you something special." He turned away to make the drink. "Because," he continued under his breath, "your wife's such a fat, ugly pig."

"Excuse me?" said Cartwright.

"What?" said Wayne innocently as he filled a tall glass with straight rum. "Drink's almost ready. . . ."

"That's more like it," said Cartwright as Wayne handed over the drink.

Half an hour later, a fairly drunk Barry Cartwright scanned the dance floor. His glassy eyes fixed on Claire Barnes, who was dancing a pretty decent hula.

Casually, he sidled up and danced close to her. "You look very beautiful tonight," he said quietly.

"Stop teasing me," said Claire, teasing him.

"I've been watching you all night," he said.

"And what have you decided?" she asked invitingly.

"I need you," he said. "Now."

"What about your wife?"

At the buffet table, Mrs. Barry Cartwright was filling her plate.

"Won't even notice," her husband murmured. "She's a little preoccupied with the buffet."

"You poor thing," Claire said to Barry cutely. "You

want to sneak away somewhere?"

"Our special place," he said as he nuzzled her neck. "Five minutes?"

Claire looked around conspiratorially. "Can't wait," she whispered.

Cartwright gently brushed against her as he walked past.

A few minutes later, he was walking up the path toward the fourth green, whistling. He carried a blanket, a bottle of champagne, and two glasses. The fourth green was one of the golf club's prettiest spots, being situated next to a beautiful lake with a fountain.

He did not know it, but Cartwright was not alone. From the dark body of water, a pair of luminescent blue-green eyes was watching. Their gaze lingered on Cartwright as he spread the blanket under a beautiful tree, waiting for Claire.

While he waited, he popped open the bottle, accidentally spraying champagne all over the front of his pants. "Dammit," he swore.

He walked over to the lake, took a handkerchief from his pocket, and dipped it into the water.

The luminescent eyes were fixed hungrily on Cartwright. They moved closer to him in the water.

Cartwright dabbed his champagne-stained pants with his wet handkerchief. He looked down at the spot disapprovingly. "That's going to stain," he said to himself.

As he moved to stick the handkerchief in the water again, a set of jaws opened, and two rows of strange, horrible teeth glistened brightly in the moonlight.

"Barry!" Claire called from across the green. "Barry, where are you? I can't see anything."

Cartwright pulled his hand away and turned briefly to look for her. "Over here, my pet," he called. "By the water."

He turned back to the lake, stuck the handkerchief in, and—

Whomp! Chomp! The awful jaws snapped shut, snatching the handkerchief right out of his hand.

"What the hell . . . ?" said Cartwright.

In a fraction of a second, before he could move away, a weird creature the size of a small alligator sprang out of the water. It latched onto Cartwright's torso with incredible ferocity.

"*Ahhhhh!*" screamed Cartwright. But the creature was attacking him like a badger, shaking his body from side to side with its powerful grip. Cartwright tried to fight, frantically grasping at the ground, but the creature was incredibly strong. In a moment, it had pulled him down into the water.

The water closed over them and grew calm, as if nothing had happened.

Now Claire arrived. In the pale moonlight, she looked at the blanket and the champagne, and she smiled. "Oh, Barry, you're so sweet," she said.

She looked around. No sign of Barry.

"Barry . . ." she said. "Barry? Is this a game?"

She spotted a handkerchief floating on top of the water

and went over to the bank of the lake. "C'mon out, Barry, this isn't fun anymore," she said petulantly.

As she got closer, she noticed that the handkerchief was covered with blood.

Then Cartwright's head popped out from under the water.

Claire screamed and screamed and screamed, out of her mind with fright, as Cartwright was viciously pulled back under by the creature.

She started running, and did not look back until she had reached the pool, where the party was still in full, oblivious swing. Music was blaring, people were dancing, Wayne was serving drinks.

In stormed Claire, issuing an ear-piercing shriek. The music stopped. All eyes focused on her. She was shoeless and her dress was half undone. "Something just ate Barry Cartwright!" she screamed.

Nobody was looking at Wayne right then, but there was an interesting look on his face.

● ● ●

In the research facility, Ira and Allison were having a cup of coffee in the cafeteria.

"What were you thinking, going into the cave like that?" said Allison.

"We were desperate. Look, I teach biology at a community college in northern Arizona. I'm not likely to get close to anything remotely as significant as this for the rest of my career. When your friends broke into our lab—I don't know, it seemed like a good idea at the time." He looked down into his coffee. "Thanks for not calling the cops," he finished humbly.

She looked at him, shaking her head. "I'm sure Harry will be fine," she said. "Of course, what do I know? I'm just a humorless geek with deep-seated neuroses—in dire need of some good loving."

Busted! "You heard that, huh?" said Ira sheepishly.

"Oh, I heard it all right." She took a sip of her coffee. "I'm a longtime fan of yours, you know," she said.

Ira looked at her, surprised.

"I wrote my senior thesis on you. Well, on your work, anyway."

Ira was shocked. "Your college thesis?" he said. "Please, we're practically the same age."

"'Predicting Protein Structure in Genetic Networks—An Analysis of Dr. Ira Kane's Early Research on G Protein Receptors,'" Allison recited with a chuckle.

"Catchy title," grinned Ira.

Allison smiled, charmed. "You got me into infectious diseases," she told him.

"If I had a dime for every time I heard that," Ira said, goofing. Allison laughed.

But now Ira grew serious. "Allison," he said, "the changes in the cave . . . in just two weeks—it's shocking."

"Yes," Allison agreed. "They're growing exponentially."

"And I wouldn't take comfort from their present inability to tolerate oxygen," he went on. "These things are vicious and dangerous."

"The only thing dangerous around here," said a voice behind them, "is you, Ira." It was Woodman. He looked like someone who had just been summoned out of bed.

"Russell," said Allison. "What are you doing here?"

"Flemming woke me," he replied. He glanced at Ira in disgust. "I didn't realize we were giving coffee to felons these days."

"Speaking of felonies," said Ira without missing a beat, "were there any more hard drives you were planning to erase?"

This got him an icy stare from Woodman. "Now you listen to me, Ira Kane," he said. "You are trying my patience here. I could have you and your idiot partner thrown in jail for the stunt you pulled tonight."

"But there's been no harm done," Allison said quickly, "and Dr. Kane has given me his personal assurance that it won't happen again."

"I want you and your friend off this base immediately," Woodman told Ira. "And if I ever see you here again, I assure you the next time there'll be bars between us. You got that?"

CHAPTER TEN

The next morning, when Harry's Jeep pulled up to the science building at the community college, Wayne's beat-up car was sitting out front.

"So," Harry said to Ira as they got out of the car, "what's with you and the first lady of science? You get any action while I was in recovery?"

Ira rolled his eyes. "Yeah," he said. "Didn't you see it on the monitors?"

But before Harry could go any farther with the joke he noticed a familiar-looking old Cutlass parked outside the lab. "We've seen that car before," he told Ira.

When they walked into Ira's messy office, who should be standing there but Wayne. He was holding a large sack.

"Hey, it's the meteor guy," said Harry.

"You know," said Wayne, "I was thinking of taking some classes here. But I decided to enter the job market early and get a jump on things."

"Can I help you?" said Ira.

Wayne got right down to business. "A guy got killed at my country club last night," he said. "A real moron—but that doesn't make it right, you know?"

"So?" said Harry.

Wayne plopped the heavy sack down on the desk. "It was an animal attack," he continued. "Happened by the water hazard on the fourth green. The lady he was messing around with saw the whole thing. Anyhow, we drained the pond and chased this thing around the fairway. Then it died in a sand trap, like it was choking to death."

He opened the sack and dumped the dead creature onto the desk. "It's like nothing I ever saw before. Thought you guys might want to have a look."

Ira and Harry were now paying attention.

● ● ●

Allison had just stepped out of the shower in her room at the Ramada in downtown Glen Canyon. She was shaking the water out of her hair when she heard a loud knocking at her door. She uttered an oath under her breath; why did this only happen when she was soaking wet?

Wrapping a towel around her, she walked to the door and opened it.

Ira was standing on the other side. His eyes opened a bit wider when he saw her in the towel, her body and hair still wet. "I seem to be seeing an awful lot of you lately," he said.

"What are you doing here?" she said crabbily.

"They're spreading," said Ira.

This did draw a curious look from Allison.

"There was an attack at the Mesa Verde Country Club last night," he explained. "A death. A pool guy there, Wayne, brought us the creature. Its DNA checked out—it's extraterrestrial."

"Could it be an anomaly?" she asked him. "A one-time occurrence?"

"I don't think so," said Ira. He moved a little closer to her. "Can I come in?"

"No, you can't come in. I'm half-naked here."

Ira stepped into the room anyway. "I promise not to look this time," he said.

"Didn't the guy who found the meteor work at Mesa Verde?" she asked him. "Maybe he accidentally transported a spore or something."

"It's possible," he said. "But he never actually came in contact with the rock." Ira looked around at her standard, middle-of-the-road hotel room. "This is the room the government puts you up in?" he said. "I'm glad I'm in the private sector."

"You work at a community college," she said, exasperated.

He took an apple from a fruit basket on the table, sniffed it, and took a bite as he sat down on the bed, making himself comfortable.

"What are you doing?" she said.

"I'm sitting down. I've been up for forty-eight hours."

"Get off my bed," she ordered.

"C'mon . . ." Ira wheedled.

Allison took him firmly by the arm. "Let's go," she said.

True to Allison's awkward form, though, the towel slipped a couple of inches as she pulled him up. She quickly yanked it back up.

Ira was still trying. "What kind of moisturizer do you use?" he asked. "It's so dry here and your skin is so smooth. . . ."

"Out," she said, leading him to the door.

"Allison, don't take this lightly," he said, his tone getting serious.

"I don't."

Now he was dead serious. "It's very important for us to know if there's been any breach in our efforts to isolate these creatures," he said. "Because their arrival here probably isn't just about evolution. It's evolution with a purpose."

"What purpose?"

"Displacement," he said.

"Excuse me?"

"Panspermia," Ira said. "The old germ theory. Spores land, propagate, evolve . . . displace."

"I'm an epidemiologist, Ira," Allison said. "I know what panspermia is."

"Then you must see what I'm getting at. They're not here to visit. They're moving in."

"Yeah? Well, we were here first."

"Tell that to the dinosaurs," said Ira. He looked worried—really worried. "Look," he went on, "I don't know what this is. Maybe it's an isolated incident. Frankly, I'm so bleary-eyed right now I'd believe anything. But if this is real . . ."

"All right," said Allison, making a snap decision. "I'll go back to the compound and brief Woodman about this. We'll sink some sensors in the outlying areas."

"And a satellite thermal scan," added Ira as he reached the door. "That'll give us a clearer picture of what's happening."

"Fine," she agreed.

He stuck his head back in as Allison was about to close the door. "Can't we just cuddle for a few minutes?" he begged.

She closed the door behind him, trying to suppress a smile.

● ● ●

That same morning, in the Glen Canyon suburb of Valley Vista, a Mary Kay cosmetics sale was in progress at Jill Mason's smallish, tidy house. Valley Vista was a housing tract, carved into a hilltop that looked over the Arizona desert. It was just a few miles from the cavern where the meteor had struck.

Four women—Jill, Patty, Debbi, and Grace—were sitting around Jill's living room, inspecting the cosmetic samples that were strewn everywhere. Patty, dressed in a pink skirt and jacket, was conducting the sale.

Patty opened a small vial and let her friends sniff the contents. "It contains a space-age formula for that little bit of extra help we can all use around the eyes, if you know what I mean," she said.

Grace dabbed some on her face. "Oh, this feels nice," she said. "Tingly. How much did you say it was?"

"Well," said Patty, "it's ten dollars for the large bottle, but I can sell you the sample vials at a dollar apiece if you're not sure."

Grace mulled this over. "Oooh . . . a dollar? I don't know . . ."

Jill rolled her eyes, then grabbed Grace's pocketbook from her. She fished out a couple of dollar bills and handed them to Patty. "Here," she said. "She'll take two."

Debbi, a portly woman, was hunting around the trays of finger sandwiches. The only ones left were cucumber. "Hey," she said, "are there any more of those little ham sandwiches?"

"There should be a tray in the kitchen," Jill told her.

"Would you like some of the cream first?" Patty asked Debbi.

"Oh, none for me, thanks," said Debbi, walking out of the room. "Don't seem to have a problem with wrinkles."

"She has her own miracle formula," Jill said quietly to the others. "It's called Krispy Kreme."

They laughed meanly as Debbi headed down the hallway toward the kitchen.

When Debbi got to the kitchen, she glanced down at the floor. There, near the baseboard, was a line of small, dead bugs.

"Hoofah!" she exclaimed, waving away the stench that emanated from the insects. "You've got some kind of infestation here, Jill!" she called.

"Huh?" said Jill from the living room.

Debbi was now following the line of little dead creatures along the baseboard. It appeared that they'd come from a closet in the hallway. "Jill, you have a serious bug problem!" she yelled.

Then she heard something from the closet. *Thump . . . thump thump*, it went. It was a sort of banging noise, accompanied by what sounded like wheezing.

"Jill?" Debbi called nervously. "There's something in your closet!"

"What?"

Now Jill and the others came to join Debbi in the hallway. *Thump . . . thump . . .*

The four of them stood nervously in front of the door.

"What do you keep in there?" Patty asked Jill.

"You know, the water heater and some of Joe's old crap."

There was more thumping, and then some wheezing.

"Open it, Grace," said Jill.

"Me?" said Grace. "It's your house."

Jill gave her a glare, and Grace gingerly opened the closet door.

They huddled around the closet, peering anxiously into the darkness.

And then, out walked the cutest creature. It looked a little like a muskrat, but with big googly eyes, wrinkly skin like a shar-pei dog's, and four short legs.

Haltingly, it stumbled into the light. The creature was trembling, shivering, and wheezing, trying its hardest to breathe but having difficulty.

"Hey, when did you guys get a dog?" Grace asked Jill.

"We don't have a dog!" Jill snapped.

"I don't think that's a dog," Debbi ventured. "It's like some kind of rodent."

"Maybe a muskrat or pig or something," said Patty.

"Well, how the hell did it get in here?" Jill said, her voice rising.

"Doesn't look too healthy, does it?" Debbi remarked.

Grace bent down to look at the creature. "It's frightened," she said. "He's probably more scared of us than we are of him. Look, he can barely breathe, he's so scared." She reached out to let it sniff her hand. "C'mon, cutie-pie," she cooed. "Don't be afraid. It's okay."

In a flash, something popped right out of the cute creature's mouth. It was a *second head*! And this head was not cute in the least. It was reptilian, grotesquely ugly, and covered in mucus. And it had a mouthful of long, daggerlike teeth.

"Jeez!" said Jill.

Quick as lightning, the second head shot forward as though it were spring-loaded, and chomped down on Grace's hand, taking a chunk of flesh with it. *"Ahhhhhhhhhhh!"* screamed Grace.

Jill ran to a drawer and pulled out a pistol as Patty dialed 911.

And then, just as Jill was about to blow the creature away, it started choking and convulsing on the ground. Then it suddenly dropped dead.

Stunned, the four women stared at its lifeless body.

● ● ●

In a booth at the Glen Canyon Coffee Shop, Harry and Wayne were enjoying a hearty breakfast.

"So," Harry was saying, "I've been an adjunct professor going on four years now, but I'm hoping this whole alien brouhaha will net me an honorary doctorate somewhere." He pointed to Wayne's plate. "You gonna eat those potatoes?"

"Yeah, I'm gonna eat them. I ordered them, didn't I?" said Wayne. "What about the coaching? Girls' volleyball? Do you get to see the team in the shower?"

"Yeah, sure, all the time. Sometimes I go in and shower with them."

Wayne looked at Harry unsurely. "You're kidding me, right?" he said.

Ira arrived and sat down in the booth.

"Did she buy it?" Harry asked him eagerly. "You weren't the shy guy, were you?"

"She's gonna talk to Woodman," Ira answered. "And no, I was not shy." He looked for the waitress. "Can I get a cup of coffee?" he called out.

She came over and poured a cup of coffee for Ira. But when Ira went to pour some cream in his coffee, he noticed that the cream container was empty.

Ira turned to the table next to them. "Can I borrow your cream?" he asked, without taking much of a look at the occupants.

Then Ira realized who he was speaking to. It was Denise, his ex. She was having breakfast with a good-looking police officer: Sam Johnson, one of the cops who had been guarding the crash site.

"*Denise?*" said Ira.

"Hello, Ira. Still setting the world on fire?" she asked sarcastically.

"Well, yes," he replied. "I happen to be working on a very big project. What's with the police escort?"

"This is Sam," she said. "He's about to make detective."

Now Ira recognized Sam. "Hey, Sam," he cracked, "perhaps you can look into what happened to my shirts."

"See what I mean?" Denise said to Sam. She turned back to Ira. "Here, want your shirt?" she said, and started taking the shirt off her back. "Take it, you freak."

"Let's all calm down," said Sam. "I'm sure he'll let you borrow the shirt for today. Nice to see you, Dr. K."

Just then, Sam's radio went off. "Uh . . . ten-niner-niner," said the dispatcher's tinny voice, "we've got a code one-two-seven-two over in Valley Vista. . . ."

"One-two-seven-two—that's an animal attack," Wayne told Ira and Harry in a low voice.

Sam picked up his radio. "Ten-nine-nine responding," he said into it.

He stood up, taking a last bite of toast. "Gotta go, babe," he said to Denise. He gave her a kiss.

"Some kind of animal problem?" Ira asked Sam.

"Yeah," Sam replied. "Up at Valley Vista."

"Hey," Denise said to Sam as he put on his hat. "Be careful out there."

Denise turned to Ira as Sam made his way out of the coffee shop. "He actually cares about the world," she said spitefully.

Ira turned to the guys, ignoring her.

"This has kind of an ominous feel, doesn't it?" said Wayne quietly.

"Let's check it out," Ira said.

Throwing some bills on the table, they got up and followed Sam out of the coffee shop.

"He cares about the world," Harry said to Denise in a mocking voice as they left.

- - -

Inside the huge dome of the research compound, Allison was arguing with Woodman as they walked toward the control room.

"I advise you not to have anything to do with that charlatan," Woodman was scolding her, "and first thing you do is entertain him in your hotel room? C'mon, Allison, you're smarter than that."

"Okay, first of all, Russell," she said, "I wasn't entertaining anyone. I don't even know anyone who still uses that term. Secondly, you're missing the point here. These damn things are spreading."

"You're referring to the attack at the golf course?" said Woodman.

"Yes," said Allison, clearly surprised that he knew.

"We're already on it," he said. "I've sent in a team to clean things up. It's an isolated incident, probably organisms brought in by that pool guy. Nothing to worry about."

"Let's be sure. Order up some deep sensors and a satellite scan. Let's just be safe."

"We've got it under control," Woodman said curtly. "Thanks, though."

He walked off with an air of finality.

When she reached the control room, Allison approached Cryer, who was manning the control panel. "Cryer," she said, "do me a favor. Have your men sink a half-dozen new sensors at the outlying areas. Deep ones, fifty feet or so. And order a satellite-based thermal scan of the region."

"I'll need approval for that," he told her.

"I'm approving it," she said.

Cryer looked uncomfortable, hating to be caught in the middle. "I'm gonna catch a lot of heat if Woodman finds out," he said.

"I'll take the heat," said Allison sweetly. "C'mon, I need this."

Just out of sight, behind a bank of monitors, Flemming stood watching them.

CHAPTER ELEVEN

When Harry's Jeep pulled up in front of Jill Mason's house, there were already two squad cars outside the house. And then, as Harry and Ira climbed out of the Jeep, a TV news van with a satellite dish pulled up across the street.

Ira eyed the news van. "Looks like we're under a microscope here," he said. "Let's be very systematic and subtle about what we do. No cowboy stuff."

"No problem," said Harry.

"Professionals," agreed Wayne.

When the three of them got to the top of the front steps, they found Sam Johnson taking a statement from Jill Mason.

"What are you doing here?" Johnson asked them, surprised.

"We heard about the animal attack," said Ira.

"And part of our job with the college and State Health Department," Harry explained, "is to ascertain if there's any health risk to others."

"Hope you didn't touch it with your bare hands," Ira said.

"That would be a serious no-no," said Harry.

"Okay—sure, come in," said Johnson, stepping aside from the doorway.

"So," said Ira as he moved past Johnson, "how long have you and Denise been seeing each other?"

Johnson just gave him a look.

Inside, Ira, Harry, Jill, and two cops stood with their shirts covering their noses, looking into the closet at the dead "cutie-pie" animal.

"In a world full of putrid odors, this one takes the cake," said Harry, trying not to retch.

Ira found an old rowboat oar and used it to start digging through the closet. As he moved away all the household junk, he could begin to see that the floor of the closet was unfinished. The small room sat directly over the bare earth.

"It's just for storage," Jill explained. "And access under the house."

"It must have come out of the dirt," Ira mused. "We're at least two miles from the cave; how'd it get all the way out here?"

The sliding glass door from the backyard opened, and Wayne stuck his head in. "I was conducting a perimeter check," he said to his companions. "You might want to check this out."

Harry followed Wayne toward the steep hill in the Masons' backyard. "If you liked the alligator thing," said

Wayne, "you're gonna love this."

When they got to the crest of the hill, Harry saw something the likes of which he'd never seen before. Nobody on earth, in fact, had ever seen anything like this before.

Stretched out before him was a broad valley, and the valley was strewn with dozens of dead alien creatures.

The creatures were big. Aliens this size that had not been seen, in the cave or anywhere else. They were hideous monsters, each one slightly different, but all huge and birdlike. They had coarse tendrils of different colors, deep crimson eyes, and jagged, spiky teeth. There were dead alien monsters as far as the eye could see.

"Well, I'll be," said Harry.

- - -

In a little while, Ira, Harry and Wayne were walking through the Valley of the Dead Alien Birds. "And to think," said Ira wryly, "I once dreamed of owning a vacation home here."

Close up, the things were even more hideous. They looked like huge reptilian hyena-birds. Some of them were half-buried in the ground, as if they had choked to death as soon as they'd come out and hit the air. Above them, the three men could see that here was a deep opening in the slope below the houses.

"They're crawling out, trying to adapt to our atmosphere," said Ira. "Fortunately, they haven't. So far."

"I think I know how these things got here," Harry said.

"How?" Ira asked him.

"This entire area's a honeycomb of caves and old mine shafts," said Harry. "If memory serves, the Moenave cave system starts a few miles from here, just west of the golf course, and runs into the foothills just below the Kaibab Plateau." He pointed into the distance. "It continues almost as far as Lake Powell," he said. "Our cave is smack-dab in the middle of the system."

"I'm impressed," said Ira.

"Hey, underneath this casual exterior beats the heart of a scientist," said Harry.

There was some movement on the ground near Wayne. He bent down to look. "That one's moving," he said, pointing at one of the hyena-birds.

It was rolling around on the ground. Then, slowly, breathing with difficulty, it got up on two wobbly legs and began moving around, looking shaky.

"It's trying to breathe," said Ira, fascinated.

The bird-thing started choking and writhing around. Then it began to cough, as if it had something in its throat.

Suddenly, the creature vomited a mucus-covered pod out of its mouth.

"Yeech," said Harry.

"I don't know if I really need to see this," said Wayne.

Then, as the three of them stood by, gaping, the pod unfurled itself into a struggling alien bird.

"Mazel Tov!" joked Harry. "It's a boy!"

The creature had little mucus-covered green sacs on its neck—sacs that expanded and contracted.

It was breathing.

The new, improved alien extended its massive wings and let out an ear-shattering *AAAAAARRRRKKK!*

"Oh, God," said Ira, "it's oxygen-tolerant."

They watched it fly off. "Oh, fabulous," said Ira, in a tone that was anything but excited.

"It's bad that it's flying away, isn't it?" said Harry, following it with his eyes.

"C'mon!" Ira yelled. "We can't lose track of it!"

They all ran for the car.

In a few minutes, Harry's Jeep was hurtling down Glen Canyon Road at ninety miles an hour. It lifted into the air as it cleared a hill, and landed with a bone-jarring thud. While Harry concentrated on driving, Ira and Wayne looked out of the Jeep's open top, trying to spot the flying, breathing alien creature.

"Do you see it?" said Harry.

"No!" Ira shouted into the wind.

"You'd think it'd be pretty easy to spot," Wayne said to Ira. "You know, being a flying alien and all."

"So let me get this straight," said Harry as he wrestled with the wheel. "They now breathe air, they're vicious as hell, and they're multiplying like yuppies on fertility drugs.

What's to keep them from, say, oh I don't know, eating us?"

Ira gave him a look. "Not much," he said.

They heard it before they saw it. That terrible, screeching cry: *AAAAARRRRKKKK!*

Like a huge aircraft, the winged monster rose into the air from behind a nearby hill. It soared across the sky, cutting across their path.

"Over there!" yelled Wayne, pointing.

"Where's it going?" said Harry.

● ● ●

In the local mall, shoppers searched for bargains at the department store while Muzak played in the background.

A plump middle-aged cashier, way too cheery for her own good, was counting out change for a customer. "Seven, eight, forty-five, fifty . . ." she said, putting the money in the customer's hand. "You're gonna love that housecoat, by the way. I've got two myself. Course, we do get a substantial discount. You have yourself a great day. Next loyal customer in line please!" she shouted out.

Crassshhh!

The next loyal customer was a gigantic alien bird, which smashed right through the huge front window of the store, shattering it into a million pieces.

Picking itself up and shaking the glass shards off its body, the bird slowly recovered from the crash. Then it let out an ear-piercing *AAAAAAAARRRRKKKKK!*

"Oh my," said the cashier.

Now the bird came flying directly toward her. She managed to dive out of the way. Pandemonium had erupted in the store as shoppers scurried for the exits, screaming. As the alien bird flew through the store, it knocked over shelves, toppled neat stacks of items, and wrecked light fixtures suspended from the ceiling.

Customers were running out of the store, screaming as they jumped into their cars. The parking lot was a mess, with cars crashing into each other as shoppers battled to get away.

This was the scene our three heroes encountered as Harry's Jeep pulled up to the store. "Think this might be the place?" asked Harry.

They scrambled out of the car and raced inside, following the screams to the sporting goods department.

A few quick but emphatic swings of a baseball bat, and Ira had broken the glass of the gun cases. He reached in and grabbed a pump-action shotgun for each of them, and a few boxes of shells.

"You know how to use one of these?" Wayne asked Harry as he loaded his gun.

"Hey, just because I'm a schoolteacher doesn't make me a wuss," Harry retorted. He shook his head. "Do I know how to use one of these. . . ."

Ira cut in. "Guys. There's a flying extraterrestrial in the store. Focus," he said.

- - -

The dressing room was empty, except for a teenage girl who was in one of the stalls, obliviously trying on T-shirts. She put one T-shirt on over another, and then another over that one, the tags still attached. Then she lifted her overalls up over the shirts and buttoned them. There. The perfect outfit for shoplifting.

She heard a noise in the hall outside her stall.

"Just finishing up in here," she said nervously. She hurried to finish dressing.

Now there was a scratching at the door.

"Gimme one minute. . . ." she said, struggling with her clothes.

Bam! Something smashed loudly on the stall door.

"Just a sec. . . ."

BAM! The banging got louder.

"I said, just a second!" yelled the girl.

BAM! The door was smashed so hard, an indentation punched through the wood.

Now the girl had really had it. "How'd you like to have the eyes scratched out of your head!" she yelled. Angrily, she yanked the door open.

And there, outside her stall, was a big surprise.

AAAARRRRKKKK! it said.

The girl's face was now a mask of terror, as the alien bird thrust its head forward and bared its nasty, daggerlike teeth.

The bird-thing lunged, grabbing her with its claws, and took off in flight. It smashed through the swinging wood doors of the dressing room area, dragging the screeching girl out of the store and into the center of the mall. Higher and higher it climbed, closer and closer to the ceiling, shattering dozens of long fluorescent lights in its wake.

Harry, Ira, and Wayne spotted the bird and the girl, soaring way up near the ceiling. *AAARRRRKKKK!* shrieked the bird.

Harry aimed his gun at it. "I've got a clear shot!" he said.

"No!" cried Ira. "You'll hit the girl!"

In that instant, the bird abruptly changed direction. Now it was heading for the large open area at the other side of the mall.

"But it's flying out of the mall!" Harry said to Ira.

Looking around for another solution, Wayne noticed a display of home karaoke machines. "Maybe this'll work," he said to himself.

He dropped his gun, grabbed the microphone from one of the machines, and hit a button. Then, climbing up on a large speaker, he started waving his arms wildly, trying to get the attention of the alien bird.

Finally, the music from the machine kicked in. It was the instrumental track to Joe Cocker's corny hit, "You Are So Beautiful."

"You got to be kidding," said Harry, grimacing at the choice of music.

But Wayne kept singing. "You are so beautiful to me. . . . Can't you see-eee!" he wailed.

"Oh man," said Harry, watching Wayne try to sing, "that is *weak*."

Wayne continued, really putting his heart into it. He was trying desperately to communicate with the bird.

"You're everything I hoped for, you're everything I need . . ." he caterwauled.

"I've had them *inside* me," Harry yelled. "That's not gonna work!"

But, incredibly, it did work. Just as it was about to escape the mall, the alien bird made a wide turn toward them. Its beady eyes were focused curiously on Wayne.

"You are so beautiful, to me-eee," sang Wayne, as the bird swooped down, heading directly for Wayne, with the screaming girl's legs hitting the tops of the shelves.

"Get ready," said Ira.

Just as the bird was upon him, Wayne dove out of the way. Ira grabbed the girl's legs, prying her out of the alien's grip as it soared past him. He and the girl both went tumbling to the floor.

The girl looked up at Ira, terror still on her face. "I'm sorry, I'm so sorry," she blubbered, "I'll never shoplift again."

The hyena-bird was still in flight, and Ira was still holding his gun. In a moment, the thing swooped right over him and into his sights.

Blam! Blam! Blam! Blam! He fired, spraying it with gun-shot. A direct hit.

The alien bird fell like a stone, plummeting straight into a big Thanksgiving diorama of Pilgrims and Indians sharing a turkey feast. It was just perfect.

Harry and Wayne were pumped. They looked at Ira, whose shotgun was still smoking.

"You enjoy that as much we did?" said Wayne.

"Yeah," said Ira. "We should go out—do this more often."

Harry grinned, pointing at Ira and singing: "Bad boys, bad boys, whatcha gonna do. . . ."

CHAPTER TWELVE

Out behind Jill Mason's house, in the Valley of the Dead Alien Birds, things were hopping. The police and the military had cordoned off the area on the ground, while a TV news helicopter circled above, getting shots of the valley. Now the whole television-viewing public in northern Arizona was in on the government's little secret.

Up in the helicopter, a traffic reporter was doing his best to describe the situation below for the at-home audience. It was different from his usual fare of traffic jams and jack-knifed tractor-trailers. "We're going to try to zoom in a little closer here. . . ." he said.

"Uh, Tom," said the news anchor, "could you describe again what we're seeing, for those viewers who've just joined us?"

The camera moved in tighter on one of the dead alien birds.

"Okay," said Tom, delivering his voice-over. "We're directly above Valley Vista, where I'd say there were about a hundred or so giant dead creatures. They certainly don't look like anything I've ever seen before. . . ."

"Tom, let's stress to our viewers," the anchor interrupted, "that we have, to this point, received no official confirmation from the Arizona Fish and Wildlife Bureau as to the origin of the creatures, rumors about aliens notwithstanding."

● ● ●

Not far away, at a road-work site that was out on a remote stretch of Arizona desert, things were also quite busy. News vans with satellite dishes on their roofs crowded the area around the work site.

A news reporter was interviewing a road-crew guy on camera. "All's I saw," said the road worker, "was an ugly tentacle thing reach up from the ground and try to grab me, right between the legs. It pulled the jack hammer right under." The guy pointed to a bandaged wound on his leg. "It's ugly, I'll tell ya that."

● ● ●

By late that afternoon, the State Capitol Building was also swarming.

Sherry Blanch, an abrasive TV reporter, was standing amid a sea of press, talking on camera.

". . . with confirmed attacks pouring in by the hour," she said feverishly into the mike, "one of the strangest days in Arizona history draws to a close. And still, silence from the governor's office. The absence of any official word from state authorities has created an atmosphere of confusion and anxiety in the greater Glen Canyon area."

— — —

Back in the research compound, Woodman was watching Sherry Blanch's report on one of the television monitors inside the tent.

"And so," the reporter was concluding, "we wait outside the State Capitol Building for any comment from the governor's office concerning the origin and nature of these extraordinary creatures."

Flemming approached Woodman with a freshly printed satellite photo in hand. "You might want to see this," he said.

Woodman took the photo from him.

"The red areas," Flemming explained, "show a distinct pattern of thermal increases, moving out concentrically from the cavern. They're spreading, sir."

Woodman frowned at the photo. "I didn't order this," he said.

"It was Lieutenant Cryer," said Flemming. "Under Dr. Reed's authority."

Woodman raised an eyebrow, and then refocused on the photo. "Looks like we may have been somewhat conservative in our estimation of the danger here," he said.

"Yes, sir. Very conservative."

"Damn," said Woodman. "The president's chief science advisor just called."

"And the governor of Arizona is on his way," Flemming informed him.

"Oh, great," said Woodman. "Any more dignitaries

arriving to witness the end of my career?"

"General," said Flemming carefully, "there may be an opportunity here we haven't accounted for. . . ."

"Get to the point," said Woodman.

"When you discover a revolutionary genetic mechanism, you get to be head of U. S. Army Research."

"I'm already head of Research," Woodman reminded him.

"Yes. My point exactly, General. But—you eradicate a deadly alien threat with a massive show of force, that's the kind of thing the military respects. A general who does that, well, there's no telling how far he might go."

Woodman finally understood what Flemming was getting at. "Yes," he said, smiling. "We all love a good war, don't we?"

- - -

In a few minutes, the dust surrounding the helicopter landing zone was whipped up by the arrival of a new chopper. It carried the governor of Arizona, Frank Lewis.

Lieutenant Cryer ran up to greet him as he climbed out. "Welcome to the site, Governor Lewis," he said. "General Woodman's expecting you."

Cryer hustled the governor and his aides into the meeting room inside, where Allison, Woodman, and Flemming were already sitting around a table that was littered with satellite photos, thermal scan readouts, and reams of data.

"Somebody here want to tell me why I was not informed that there are aliens in my goddamn state?" the governor demanded. "I got four hundred media vultures camped outside my office and they know more than I do! I oughta throw all you in prison. State prison, not that cushy federal crap with the jumpsuits."

"I'm sorry, Governor," said Woodman. "But there were some earlier security breaches by Dr. Kane and his team. We thought it best to keep a tight lid on the situation. Issues of national security, you understand."

"That's not exactly true," Allison began, giving Woodman a look.

"I believe the governor's question was directed at me, Dr. Reed," snapped Woodman.

"Hey! I'm not interested in your bureaucratic crapola!" barked the governor. "I wanna know how bad this really is!"

"It's bad," answered Woodman. "The results from the new sensors and the satellite thermal scans indicate a potential problem."

"What problem?" said the governor. "Somebody better give it to me straight."

Allison walked over to a computer image that was projected onto a screen. It showed a map of the United States, with a red area surrounding Glen Canyon.

"The red markings in these projections," she said, "indicate growth of the alien ecosystem. Unless we do something immediately, we'll lose Glen Canyon in three days."

"What? Good God!" exclaimed Governor Lewis.

Now Allison hit a button, and the red area started growing. "In a week," she continued, "the rest of Arizona. . . ."

It grew some more.

"Then the entire Southwest. . . ."

The red area now covered the entire map.

"Within two months," Allison finished, "the United States officially belongs to them . . . and we're extinct."

It took a moment for everyone to digest this.

"You've got to be kidding me," said the governor at last.

There was a longish silence before the governor spoke again. "I'm gonna assume you've got some pretty damn clever plan cooked up to deal with this," he said.

Just then the doors to the meeting room burst open. In marched Ira, Harry, and Wayne.

"Anybody call an exterminator?" said Harry cheerfully.

"Good," said Woodman icily. "I'm glad you're all here." He turned to Flemming. "Call the MPs," he directed. "Arrest these men."

Flemming stood up, about to dispose of them.

"Hey, we just blew a giant alien bird out of a department store," said Ira. "We're the ones cleaning up your mess, so back off." Then he held out a hand to the governor. "Governor, I'm Dr. Ira Kane, and this is Professor Harry Block."

"From the Glen Canyon Community College Science Department," said Harry.

Everyone looked to Wayne.

"Wayne Gray," he mumbled. "Uh, I took chemistry in high school."

"You're the men that made the original discovery, right?" asked Governor Lewis.

"Yes," Woodman rushed to say, "and they're also responsible for the mess we're in right now."

"What?" said Harry.

Ira knew just how Woodman worked. "Here we go," he said grimly.

"They broke into the contained area just a few days ago," Flemming told the governor. "Breached our safety procedures—"

"And unwittingly caused the dissemination of alien organisms outside the secured area," Woodman added. "Serious criminal charges are in order."

Allison stared at Woodman. "This is all . . . garbage," she said.

"Liar, liar pants on fire," Harry sang to Woodman.

"*Shut up!*" barked the governor. "All of you. My state's about to be overrun by vicious aliens, for God's sake. We can deal with this crap later. What do we do about the big problem?"

Woodman smiled. "Well, I've already figured that out, Governor," he said.

"Well, goddamn nice of you to let me know, General!"

It was Woodman's big moment. He brought out a large map, and, using a pointer, traced a line around the alien mass. The shape of the outline, had he noticed it, was strangely reminiscent of the original single-celled organism.

"This is an outline of the infected area as of this afternoon," Woodman said. "We evacuate everyone within a five-mile perimeter. And then we blow 'em out of there."

"With what?" asked Allison, disturbed.

"Napalm," said Woodman. "Lots and lots of napalm."

"*Napalm?*" spluttered Ira. "Why don't you just nuke 'em while you're at it?" He couldn't believe they were actually thinking about using napalm. It was horrible stuff—a jelly that burst into flame when it touched flesh. As far as he knew, it hadn't been used since the Vietnam War.

Flemming was mulling over what Ira had said, though. "What about nukes?" he said.

"Nobody's dropping any A-bombs on my state!" yelled the governor. "And I gotta say, all this talk about napalm and burnin' things up is making me pretty damn nervous."

"You should be," said Ira. "On a cellular level, we have no idea how they'll respond to that kind of attack."

"It's time for a military solution, Governor," Woodman insisted. "This will work!"

Suddenly, Lieutenant Cryer stepped into the room, a look of concern on his face." Sorry to interrupt, General," he said. "You'd better take a look in the control room."

Looks of alarm traveled around the room.

They all rushed to the control room. There, on one of the video monitors, a strange apelike creature could be seen standing right in front of the camera lens. It seemed to be some sort of nasty-looking alien primate.

Then the creature slowly raised a large bone in its hand and started beating it against a tree. *Bam, bam, bam.* Over and over again the creature hit the tree.

"Bumm . . . bumm . . . bumm . . . ba-dumm!" sang Harry, doing the theme from *2001: A Space Odyssey.*

"What the hell's going on?" said Governor Lewis impatiently.

"You pulled me out for this?" Woodman said to Cryer.

"Well, sir," Cryer said, "one of these, uh . . . creatures just destroyed Video Four."

He pointed to a monitor that was filled with static.

Down in the cavern, the creature looked curiously right at the camera. Its hideous face could now be seen in close-up.

"That's a face for radio," said Wayne.

The primate suddenly lifted the stick high in the air, and—*wham!*—brought it right down onto the camera. Instinctively, they all jumped back from the monitor.

The video image faded from the monitor as it too went out of commission, and they were all left staring at a screenful of loud static.

They looked at each other, trying to comprehend. Then, one by one, each of the other monitors slowly went blank. The sound of static filled the room.

Cryer recovered first. "The monitors are all down!" he said.

"We're blind," said Allison.

"I don't like this," said the governor.

Then they heard a low rumbling noise: the sound of

the mine shaft elevator slowly ascending.

"The elevator," Ira said, spooked.

Allison looked frightened. "They've breached the air lock," she said. "Something's coming up."

"Call for backup," Woodman said to Flemming.

The elevator continued upward. They all backed away, waiting edgily as it rose.

Woodman and Cryer grabbed rifles out of the emergency cases that hung on the wall, and trained them on the elevator door.

The elevator appeared. The doors opened. There was nothing inside.

Now there were confused looks all around. "They're jerkin' us around," Wayne said slowly.

Then . . . the sound of tearing.

As one, they whipped around just as one of the primate creatures ripped through the thick plastic tarp behind them. It was using the sharp claws of a dead animal as a cutting tool.

"Oh, crap!" said Harry.

Then two others leaped out of the hole in the tarp and raced menacingly toward the governor.

"*Watch out!*" Wayne yelled.

The governor's aides, along with Woodman, ran for cover, leaving Cryer to deal with the apelike aliens. He raised his rifle and got off one shot, but he was hit by one of them almost immediately, sending his weapon flying. Meanwhile, the creatures set upon Governor Lewis, punching and kicking him, trying to rip him apart.

"Help! Get this damn thing off me!" screamed the governor.

Cryer and Wayne rushed over to help. Wayne swung a nearby folding chair, hitting one of the creatures squarely on its head. It released Lewis, turning its attention on Cryer instead.

In a flash, they had dragged the helpless lieutenant through the tarp and disappeared back down into the cavern. Cryer could be heard screaming. Then, all was quiet.

Governor Lewis picked himself off the ground just as a platoon of armed soldiers rushed into the dome. Woodman, seeing that the coast was clear, had also returned.

"I don't care what you have to do," the governor shouted at Woodman, "or how much firepower it takes. Get these goddamn things out of my state!"

"Yes, sir!" said Woodman with a triumphant smile. "We go at noon tomorrow."

As the assembled group slowly pulled themselves together, Woodman walked over to Ira. "I want you and your 'team' out of here," he ordered. "Now. This science project is over."

Now he turned to Allison. "Don't you have work to do?" he said.

"You are such an ass," replied Allison, walking away.

There was nothing for Ira, Harry, and Wayne to do but leave the compound. Totally dejected, they climbed into Harry's Jeep.

But just as they were about to pull away, they heard a voice calling after them. It was Allison, walking toward the Jeep. "Wait!" she yelled.

She caught up with them. "Room in there for one more? I'm coming with you," she said.

"Are you sure about this?" said Ira.

Allison smiled. "Who wants to be deputy director of the CDC anyway?" she said. "The real money's in the private sector."

She heaved a large case into the back of the Jeep. "This may not mean much now," she said, "but I managed to get all of your research files back, including your original samples. If we survive, at least the two of you will get credit for the discovery."

Ira gave Allison a grateful smile.

Then she climbed into the Jeep, caught her foot in the door frame—and did a header, right into Wayne's lap.

"We haven't been formally introduced," said Wayne delightedly. "I'm Wayne."

"Just don't let her drive," Harry said softly to Ira.

Ira stepped on the gas.

CHAPTER THIRTEEN

Outside the desert compound, the field of battle was quickly cleared. A huge steel slab was lowered by crane onto the hole atop the cavern, settling with a loud thud.

In Valley Vista, a National Guard truck with a speaker on top moved through the streets. "This is for your safety," said a soldier's voice over the loud PA system. "Please take only necessary possessions and all pets and leave the area immediately. Compliance is mandatory. Repeat, this is a general evacuation order." As the truck passed, residents were loading up their cars in driveway after driveway.

— — —

On the main desert road, the traffic was jammed with cars full of belongings, all leaving town. Only Harry's Jeep was headed in the opposite direction.

Harry and Ira were in the front, Wayne and Allison in the back. They were listening to a news report on the radio.

"Traffic along the evacuation routes is extremely heavy," the news reader was saying, "and Highway Patrol officials are working overtime to find alternate routes. In the mean-time, reports of sporadic incidents of panic within the evacuation areas have prompted the governor to mobilize the National Guard."

A convoy of army vehicles powered right by them.

● ● ●

In a little while, Harry's Jeep pulled onto the road that led up to the college.

They could hear pounding music coming from the campus.

"What now?" said Wayne.

They went around a bend in the road, and there it was: a huge party being held on the broad front lawn of the college's main building. Students were dancing around and music was blaring.

"That, my friends," said Harry, "is a party. Glen Canyon Community College style."

Ira, Harry, Allison, and Wayne got out of the Jeep and made their way through the party toward the science building. On the way they passed a banner hung on a van, reading, GOODBYE ARIZONA!

Students were jumping around all over the lawn, dousing each other with drinks, and dancing. If the end of the world was coming, they were going to be having a good time when it happened.

And there was Nadine, wearing a bathing suit with a Miss Arizona banner across her chest. "Hey, Professor!" she called out to Harry.

Harry stopped.

"Party with me," she said.

Harry turned to his partners. "Do you mind if I take a little tension break?" he asked. "I've been through a lot this week. I deserve a little 'me' time."

Ira gave him a dirty look.

"Rain check," Harry said to Nadine with a shrug. They walked on, Ira shaking his head.

"Mr. Kane!" called a familiar voice. Ira turned and saw the Donalds sitting on lawn chairs, stripped down to their underwear.

"Arizona's going down! Whoo-hoo!" yelled Danny.

"Whoo-hoo!" yelled Deke similarly.

"This may not be the best time for you boys to be celebrating like that," said Ira. Then he reconsidered. "Forget it," he said.

● ● ●

Finally, the four of them were settled in the biology lab, the music from the party still pulsating through the walls.

Ira bent over a petri dish full of clear fluid, scanning its surface intently. "C'mon, fellas, talk to me," he said. "There's some secret you're not telling me."

"What is that stuff, anyway?" Wayne asked him.

"It's some of the original liquid material from the meteor," said Ira.

Allison frowned. "Why hasn't it evolved like the rest?" she asked him.

108

"I'm not sure. Maybe because it's been refrigerated. Maybe because it's been sealed in an airtight case and hasn't had anything to metabolize with. I just know the answer's here somewhere."

He leaned in and talked to again to the liquid. "What is it?" he muttered.

Harry pulled a cigarette out from behind his ear and lit it. "You're starting to lose it, pal," he said to Ira.

Ira looked at Harry's cigarette. "When the hell did you start smoking?" he asked.

"I just bummed it," said Harry, tossing the match. "There doesn't seem to be much point in clean living anymore."

Nobody was looking at the match. But the match, still lit, was falling, turning end over end, flipping toward the petri dish. Where it landed.

And in a flash, the glass dish came alive. Somehow, the fire was interacting with the liquid, bubbling up in a burst of supergrowth. Within seconds, the entire surface of the lab table was covered with bright purple alien moss, little plants and lichens, and alien mushrooms, all connected together like parts of one organism.

"Holy cow," said Wayne.

"My bad," said Harry, staring at the new alien-plant wonderland.

"So much for the military option," said Ira casually.

But Allison was not so calm. "What are we gonna do, Ira?" she cried. "These things react to fire like it was Miracle-Gro."

Suddenly Ira caught on. "The napalm! Shoot!" he said.

"You better call that idiot general," said Wayne.

● - ●

The military offensive was proceeding at full tilt At the Valley of the Dead Alien Birds, soldiers equipped with flamethrowers were being deployed along the perimeter of the valley.

In Mesa Verde, trucks were arriving hourly, carrying troops and weaponry.

Tanks and heavy guns rumbled over the fairways of the golf course.

And in around the desert compound, the fuses on the napalm barrels were all being set.

The command center was now a tent in the desert, which had been set up about a mile from the compound. Woodman was there now, studying the battle maps with a group of military officers.

"That's a lot of napalm," Flemming was saying. A note of anxiety had crept into his voice.

"Yeah," said Woodman. "We're going to blow the crap out of them, then flush them out along the mine shafts. We'll mop up at the edges as they run to escape the flames."

A soldier stepped into the tent. "Excuse me, General," he said, saluting. "There's an urgent call from a Ms. Reed. Says she's with the CDC. She's got something very important to tell you about the mission."

Woodman waved his hand dismissively. "Tell her I'm not

available." He gave Flemming a satisfied smile. "She made her bed. . . ." he said.

■ ■ ■

In the biology lab at the community college, Allison closed her cell phone. "He blew me off!" she said to her friends. "Can you believe it? That bastard wouldn't take my call."

"You did call him an ass," Ira reminded her.

There was a fuss out in the hallway, and the Donalds burst into the lab. They were carrying drinks for everyone.

"Hey, Mr. Kane!" said Deke. Then he noticed the lab table covered with alien life. "Whoa," he said, stopping short, "look at the desk."

"Hey, can we have that when you guys are done with it?" Danny asked.

"What are you doing here?" Ira asked them in exasperation.

Deke and Danny held up the cups. "Thought you guys could use a drink," said Deke.

"I'll take one of those," said Wayne, reaching for a cup.

"Gimme one, too," said Harry. "I just quit smoking."

"Okay," Allison said to the Donalds. "Thanks for the drinks, but we're working here."

She started ushering the Donalds to the door, but suddenly Ira saw something.

"Hold it!" he said.

"Dude, he needs us!" said Danny joyfully to Deke.

There, right on the back of Allison's shirt, staring Ira in the face, was the periodic table.

Ira approached Allison from behind and pulled at her shirt to straighten out the fabric.

"What are you doing?" she asked him, perplexed.

"Selenium . . ." said Ira.

"Keep pullin', Dr. K!" urged Deke, watching Allison's shirt with interest as it was pulled tighter by Ira.

"That's the answer—selenium," said Ira, getting excited now. "Take off your shirt," he told Allison.

"What? I don't think so," she said.

Ira pointed feverishly at her shirt. "Look," he said, "we're a carbon-based life-form." He pointed to the symbol C, the sixth element on the chart. "Move down here," he went on, "and you've found our poison: arsenic." Ira dragged his finger from the C symbol to the element two down and one to the right, the thirty-third element. Its symbol was As.

"You're tickling me," giggled Allison.

"But the aliens," Ira continued, "are nitrogen-based, right?" Now he moved his finger in the same pattern, starting at N for nitrogen and moving two down and one to the right, to arrive at Se.

"Selenium," said Allison.

"It should be as lethal to them as arsenic is to us," Ira said in triumph.

He finally let go of her shirt. Allison turned, which brought their faces to within inches of each other.

"And with their metabolic rates," she said, as excited now as Ira, "it'll kill them fast."

Harry snapped right to it. "Okay!" he said. "Selenium. How much do we need?"

"Five hundred gallons," guessed Ira. "Give or take."

"It's two in the morning," said Wayne. "I hate to be a buzzkill, but where do we get that at two A.M.?"

"No problem," said a cheery voice from the back of the room. It was Deke.

"Yeah, we can help you there," Danny agreed.

They all turned incredulously to the Donalds.

"Head and Shoulders," said Deke. He looked quite pleased with himself.

"The *dandruff* shampoo?" said Harry.

"That's the one. Main ingredient, selenium sulfide lotion."

Ira was totally nonplused. "How'd you know that?" he said to Deke. "You don't know anything!"

"Dr. K," said Danny, "haven't you ever noticed how shiny and flake-free our hair is?"

Ira smiled kindly at them. "You've just earned your A's," he said.

Danny started to cry, and Deke enveloped him in a big hug.

CHAPTER FOURTEEN

As the sun rose above the horizon, two cars loaded with students screeched to a halt in front of the science building. Already sitting out front was a shiny red hook-and-ladder truck, and beside the truck was a huge pile of empty shampoo bottles.

The Donalds were helping Wayne fill the tank of the fire truck with shampoo, by means of a large funnel that was sticking out of the nozzle. Grabbing more cases of the stuff, the students who had just arrived quickly formed a shampoo brigade, passing the bottles forward and helping to empty them into the funnel.

"Okay," yelled Wayne, checking the gauge. "We're full!"

Harry, Ira, and Allison were making final checks of the truck. Like Wayne and the Donalds, they were all decked out in full yellow firemen's uniforms. They looked like heroes. They looked ready for action.

"Ready?" said Ira to others.

"*Battle stations!*" yelled Harry.

As the gathered students cheered, the six boarded the fire

truck. Wayne was behind the wheel, with Ira and Allison in the cab with him. Harry manned the steering wheel at the back. The Donalds hung off the sides, like real firemen.

The engine roared to life.

"Let's go shampoo us some aliens!" yelled Ira.

● ● ●

The fire truck sped through the desert, siren blaring, kicking up a cloud of dust behind it.

As they got closer to the crash site, in the distance, they could see that a huge number of military personnel who were mobilized and preparing for the noon "isolate and destroy" mission.

"Lots of soldiers around," Wayne remarked.

"There's an old abandoned silver mine about half a click south of here," said Harry. "We can pop into the cave through there."

"Half a click?" Ira echoed. "What are you, in Vietnam?"

"Lay off, I'm diggin' this." Harry grinned.

When they got to the old mine shaft, Wayne parked the hook-and-ladder near the entrance. Ira crouched down and peered inside the dark entrance.

"You're sure this'll lead us back to the main cave?" he asked Harry.

"Well, it'll definitely lead us somewhere," said Harry nonchalantly.

Ira gave him a look.

"Hey, geology isn't an exact science," said Harry.

Meanwhile, behind them, Allison was climbing down out of the cab of the fire truck. Unfortunately, she misjudged the distance to the ground, causing her to take an unintentional header. "I'm okay!" she said, collecting herself from the ground. Wayne and the Donalds started hauling the hose toward the cave.

They were ready to go in. It was time for the Big Show.

The six of them made their way through the dark tunnel, which was lit only by their flashlights. Harry took the lead. Deke and Donald were each carrying pickaxes. Wayne and Ira pulled the hose.

Deep into the mine shaft, Harry stopped. "Shhhh!" he said, putting a finger to his lips. He was totally focused, like a tracker searching for a sign.

"Where are you?" he said quietly, touching the cave wall. "Where are you, my little aliens?"

As the rest of them watched, he ran his hand down the length of the wall.

"Warm to the touch . . ." he said, thinking. He took his hand away, sniffed it, and then licked his finger.

"Highly acidic," he said.

"Please, Harry," said Ira impatiently, "we don't have time for you to pretend like you know what you're doing."

Harry turned. "Okay," he said. "Here."

"You're sure?" said Ira.

"Hey," said Harry, "what happened to the respect?"

Ira looked hard at him, and then turned to the Donalds.

"Here," he said. "Make a big hole."

"We're gonna do you proud, Dr. K," said Deke.

Eagerly, the Donalds hoisted their pickaxes and start pounding away at the rock with all their prodigious strength, sending large hunks of rock flying.

● ● ●

Above them, in the desert, Woodman and his officers were gathered at the command post where the military operation was being coordinated.

"Are the troops in place?" Woodman said.

Flemming nodded. "Ahead of schedule," he said, pleased with himself.

"Where's the fire?" said a voice behind them. "How come I'm not seeing any fire?"

Woodman turned to find the governor and his entourage entering the tent.

He smiled coldly. "Just getting ready to start, Governor Lewis," he said. "Didn't know you were going to join us for the show."

"You damn well better make it a good one, Sergeant," said the governor.

"That's 'General,'" said Woodman, miffed.

"Not if you screw this up," returned the governor.

● ● ●

In the underground cavern, the Donalds had just finished punching the hole. The group cautiously stepped through.

They were inside the main cavern. Harry had done it!

They stood there for a moment, gaping at the sight before them. The world in the cavern had evolved into a darker and far more foreboding place. It was now a hostile alien jungle-land, where only the most vicious and hardy creatures had stood the evolutionary test of survival.

The team stepped in carefully, Ira sniffing the air as he moved through it. "Oxygen," he said grimly.

"They've done it," said Allison. "They've completely adapted. If displacement is their objective, they've just removed the last obstacle."

"Not exactly," said Wayne. He held the fire hose aloft like King Arthur brandishing his sword. "*We're* the last obstacle," he said.

"Oh, he's good," said Harry admiringly.

"Get up top," Ira said to Wayne. He turned on his walkie-talkie. "When I give you the signal, start pumping the selenium."

Wayne nodded, and was gone.

The others began making their way through the jungle, with Ira in the lead, chopping away at the growth with a machete. But this was no ordinary jungle. The air was filled with hissing, baying, and barking. Ira cut a limb off a tree, and it fell to the ground and scurried away under its own power.

Alien bird-mammals flew above; creatures the size of raccoons scurried like insects on the ground; trees moved their tendril-like branches with the dexterity of animals.

Allison stopped, hearing a rustling from above. She

looked up, but there was nothing to be seen.

Ira eyed the menacing, alien jungle around them. High above them, hidden in the trees, he saw the obscure figures of a couple of primatelike creatures. Their eyes glowed behind the unearthly foliage as they watched the group's every move.

"They're staring at us," whispered Allison uneasily.

"Maybe they're just curious," said Deke. He didn't look as if he believed it.

As they moved forward, they could hear and see the primate creatures moving with them.

Then . . . the sound of a stick banging.

Ira and Allison exchanged an apprehensive look.

There was more banging, and then more still. The other primates were joining in, pounding in unison, quietly at first but building in volume and intensity. It was beginning to sound almost like a rhythmic war march.

"Dr. K, those things are really starting to spook me out," said Danny.

Harry looked really jumpy. "Can't we just dump the stuff right here and get the hell out?" he said.

"For the selenium to work its way completely up the food chain," Ira said, "we've got to poison the simplest cells first. The ones closest to the meteor."

Ira pointed to the meteor, which was covered in the lushest and brightest growth in the cave. It was about thirty yards away.

The banging grew to a crescendo as our group stepped

closer to the meteor. Then the primates were on the move, arranging themselves between the humans and the meteor, blocking it. They were protecting the meteor.

"They're cutting us off," said Allison.

She and the others stopped moving forward. The primates held their ground. It was a Mexican standoff.

The creatures' banging was now deafening.

Then, one of the primates slowly pointed at Ira. It let out a bloodcurdling scream.

"They're going to attack!" said Harry.

Moving fast, Allison pulled a revolver from the back of her pants. She held the gun up in the air, and—*blam blam!*

The primates recoiled. The banging stopped. In the sudden silence, Ira, Harry, and the Donalds stared at Allison, amazed.

"They gave you a gun?" Harry finally said to her.

Ira leaned close to Allison. "That was so hot," he murmured into her ear.

Meanwhile, the ape-aliens were recovering. They had begun to move forward, growling.

"Do it again," Harry said to Allison.

Allison raised the gun again. But just as she was about to fire . . .

KA-BOOM . . . KA-BOOM KA-BOOOOM!

A series of massive explosions ripped through the air, going off on all sides of the cavern. The primates ran screeching away, out of their minds with terror.

Ira and Allison looked at each other, realizing what was happening. "Uh-oh," they said together.

● ● ●

Up on the surface, the barrels of napalm were exploding one by one. Huge balls of fire erupted in the desert, penetrating down into the cavern.

A little distance away, at the entrance to the mine shaft, Wayne stood by himself on the back of the hook-and-ladder, watching the napalm explosions. "What the hell?" he muttered. He glanced at his watch. "It's not noon!" he cried. "*It's not noon!*" he yelled at the explosions.

CHAPTER FIFTEEN

D own in the cavern, the group dove for cover as the entire underground ecosystem began to erupt in balls of fire.

Then they began to hear a low rumble. It was a new sound, and it was different from the napalm explosions.

"Remember that desk?" said Allison, her voice shaking.

Now, waves of heat from the fire were starting to radiate outward from the center of the cavern. At the same time, a strange fusing effect began to happen to the cave walls and floor. It was as if the pieces of rock, alien plant growth, and small animals were coming together—almost congealing.

Ira and the others dashed for the opening to the mine shaft, the cave walls and the ground underneath them beginning to shake and undulate as the fusing effect intensified. There was a fluid, almost conscious motion to the cave walls.

Ira looked back as he ran. "It's alive!" he cried.

"Yeah, everybody," said Danny helpfully, "look alive, look alive!"

"No, the cave!" said Ira. "The whole cave is alive! It's a gargantuan alien organism."

"And we're inside it!" added Allison.

They sprinted for the safety of the mine shaft and jumped inside, out of the writhing cave. But they were not out of danger yet, because the congealing effect was not confined to the cave wall. As the heat from the napalm reached the mine shaft tunnel, it too began to shudder and fuse.

● ● ●

Up on top, standing beside the pump valves of the hook-and-ladder, Wayne watched, mouth agape, as the ground around him started to move. Then it broke open. "Just keep it together, Wayne," he told himself.

Meanwhile, the fusing effect was traveling up the mine shaft walls, quickly overtaking the group as they raced for daylight at the end of the tunnel. They were in an arm of a massive creature that was coming to life around them.

The creature started to rise, and the group found that they were now running uphill. And to top it off, as the fusing effect spread, the opening at the end began to get smaller and smaller. "Shoot! It's closing up!" yelled Ira.

"I don't want to live inside the alien, Mr. Kane!" wailed Danny.

Running as fast as they could, the five of them made it to the mine shaft opening just as it was about to close. They found themselves fighting and struggling against the newly formed membrane.

In one last desperate effort, they punched through the membrane and jumped for it. They were free! Then they were falling, falling, through the air—out of what could now be recognized as a massive tentacle, rising up against the blue sky.

● ● ●

Over at Woodman's desert command center, the entire command team stood outside the tent, frozen in awe, and watched the research compound, the trucks, the dome, *everything*, falling away as the top of a huge creature came breaking out of the ground.

● ● ●

Ira and the others were running for their lives, heading toward the fire truck. The ground was shaking and rumbling all around them. Cracks were opening up in the desert floor as the huge organism rose up.

"What the hell's going on?" shouted Wayne as the group ran toward him. But there was no time for explanations. There was a mad scramble for the truck while Wayne frantically tried to gather the hose in.

"Forget the hose!" Ira yelled out to Wayne. "Just get on!" They clambered on wherever they could, Allison somehow ending up in the driver's seat.

She gunned the engine, and Wayne hopped onto the back of the truck just as it shot forward, dragging the hose behind it. The truck made a sweeping turn, sending the hose into a crazy fishtail.

"Who the hell is driving this thing?" shouted Harry,

hanging on outside for dear life.

Inside the cab, Allison was driving like a demon. But considering the circumstances, that was just what was needed.

● ● ●

Woodman's command center was in chaos. The troops were pulling back, and soldiers rushed about, barking orders over communication lines.

Governor Lewis and Woodman just stood there, staring up as the massive amoebalike creature rose up out of the ground.

"What the hell is that? What did you do?" the governor demanded to know.

"It's almost out of the ground!" Flemming reported. "It's coming this way!"

Woodman panicked. "Tell the men to shoot the damn thing down!" he ordered. "Let's turn the heat up on this thing."

● ● ●

Out at the Mesa Verde Golf Course, two old duffers named Pat and Aubrey were sneaking in one last round of golf. When they reached the thirteenth green, Aubrey's ball went into the water hazard. He put one foot into the water and lined up his shot.

As he pulled his club back, they both heard a low rumbling sound. "Did you hear that?" said Pat nervously. "We shouldn't be out here. Let's go."

"The hell I'm going," said Aubrey. "Not till I finish the front nine."

Then the ground split open.

"Holy mother of God!" cried Pat.

But it was too late to ask for help, for one of the giant tentacles was bursting out of the ground, right where Pat and Aubrey were standing.

They tried to run, but the tentacle was so huge that they were both swallowed by the earth as the tentacle rose and rose.

"Ahhhhhhhhhh!" they screamed.

And they were gone, along with the entire thirteenth hole.

● ● ●

Jill Mason's street was deserted. Her house was quiet, empty, pristine—until a block-long tentacle snaked its way up out of the ground, uprooting the houses as if they were weeds in a tiny garden. In the wink of an eye, the entire neighborhood was torn apart by the giant alien creature that was emerging from below.

● ● ●

Now the amoeba, a mile in diameter, was lumbering along, destroying everything in its path, locomoting on tentacles that stretched across the desert floor. Looked at from above, it looked remarkably like the original single-celled organisms that Ira had first found in the meteor.

Bravely, the soldiers stood their ground to shoot at it, following Woodman's orders. And with every shot, the thing got bigger. It liked the heat.

From the fire truck, which was parked behind a hill, our

six heroes watched the creature continue to grow. It was moving toward the outskirts of town.

Allison and Ira stood alone near the front of the truck.

"This is the end, isn't it?" she said.

"Looks like it," he replied bleakly.

"There's something I feel like I should tell you," she said, "but I don't know exactly how."

"Just say it. We're adults and we're gonna be dead soon anyway."

Allison nodded. "I would've rocked your world," she told him.

Ira closed his eyes, almost as if he could see what he was missing. "Yes," he said. "I bet you would've."

Harry, choosing the best possible moment, came over and joined them. "Look!" he said. "It stopped!"

They looked over at the far edge of the creature. It was undergoing a set of strange, shuddering movements that looked somehow familiar to them. Then they figured out what it was. They had witnessed before, when the cells and the flatworms had divided.

At the same time, a narrow fissure began to appear on its underside.

"Oh, God," moaned Allison. "It's splitting."

Ira was thinking, however. "This could be our chance," he said.

"What?" said Wayne.

"C'mon," said Ira. "It's time to go save the world."

— — —

A few minutes later, the hook-and-ladder truck was racing through the desert, once again kicking up dust behind it. Allison was behind the wheel, Wayne on the back, and Harry, Ira, and the Donalds manned the hose and pump mechanisms.

The fire truck approached the gigantic amoeba from behind, passing all the soldiers who were fleeing from it. Allison slowed down a bit to allow Ira to spot an opening between two of the tentacles.

"Allison, eleven o'clock," Ira shouted into the walkie-talkie. "Take us under there nice and easy."

"Check," she responded into her walkie-talkie. She steered the truck toward the gap.

Suddenly a tentacle rose up directly in front of the truck. Allison swerved hard, narrowly missing the tentacle but sending the truck into a rough skid.

"We're being attacked by a two-mile piece of Jell-O and I'm gonna die in a car accident?" shouted Harry, hanging on for dear life.

"I said nice and easy, cowboy!" Ira reminded Allison over the walkie-talkie.

But Allison was really getting into it now. "That *was* nice and easy, sweetheart!" she whooped. "Believe me, you don't want to be around when I kick it up a notch!"

CHAPTER SIXTEEN

Flemming, at the command center, was looking through his binoculars, and he spotted the fire truck driving right under the huge beast. It was a spectacular sight: a creature a mile in diameter, at least a hundred feet tall. The fire truck was minuscule in comparison, like a tiny toy. "They're out there!" Flemming cried.

"Who?" Woodman asked, trying to see.

"Kane and those wackos," Flemming replied.

"They're out of their minds," said Woodman, turning his back.

● ● ●

From the fire truck, Ira surveyed the underside of the beast. "There! *Stop!*" he yelled, pointing to a small opening. It was only about three feet in diameter, a mere speck on the bottom of the creature.

"What about 'there'?" Harry yelled back to him, trying to figure out what Ira was talking about.

Then there was a deep rumble from the creature. The large pore in the creature's underside opened briefly, letting out a stream of putrid air the likes of which had never been witnessed in the world before. The noise reverberated like a thousand tubas.

"Holy Mother in heaven!" prayed Harry.

Apparently, the hole was some sort of waste pore.

Allison, undeterred, was still on the job. She maneuvered the fire truck below the opening and stopped.

Wayne and the Donalds started to drop the stabilizers, while Ira slid over to the ladder. "Feed me the hose!" he said to the Donalds.

But just as Ira was about to step onto the ladder, he heard Harry yelling, "Wait!"

Ira turned to him.

"You?" Harry said. "Please. You've got no vertical reach. Let a brother show you how it's done."

"You sure?" Ira said.

Harry nodded. "Yeah, I've got a major score to settle."

Ira smiled.

"Hit it, Wayne!" he called out.

Wayne pulled down the lever that controlled the ladder, and it started extending upward.

The Donalds handed Harry the nozzle, and he started climbing the ladder, Ira following close behind. Higher and higher the ladder moved, with Harry holding onto hose and Ira behind him. The Donalds kept feeding the hose up.

● ● ●

With the ground rocking under them, Woodman,

Governor Lewis, and Flemming were focused on the creature.

"I recommend the nuclear option," Woodman was saying. "I'm getting the Joint Chiefs. . . ."

"What the hell are those guys doing?" asked the governor, looking through his field glasses at the fire truck.

"They seem to be getting ready to administer an extremely large enema," said Flemming with a contemptuous smile.

●　●　●

The fissure in the amoeba was still growing, the force of its splitting exerting massive pressure on the ground. It was like trying to drive in the middle of an earthquake.

"We don't have much time," yelled Allison into her walkie-talkie.

Wayne was looking up at the ladder, trying to steer it under the waste pore.

Meanwhile, up on the ladder, Harry and Ira were trying desperately to hold on. Harry slipped, and Ira extended a hand to catch him. "Thanks, man," said Harry.

Ira smiled, and then stopped smiling as he looked up at the fissure. It was still growing. "We've got one shot," he said. "Let's do this."

He got determined nod from Harry, who was making his way up the last few rungs to within inches of the creature's opening. Then, with all his might, Harry shoved the nozzle end of the hose up the creature's butt. Or whatever it was.

The Donalds opened the valves on the pump full force, and the selenium raced up through the hose and into the creature.

"Payback time!" roared Harry.

Even though the creature had no mouth or vocal cords, they could have sworn they heard a yelp.

Streams of blue liquid poured into the creature, some of it squirting out and covering Harry and Ira. As the selenium worked its way inside, the creature started shuddering, rumbling, and writhing around. Welts began bubbling up on its surface.

"Keep it in there!" Ira yelled to Harry above him.

From the cab of the fire truck, Allison was looking nervously at the beast.

"Oh, crap!" she yelled. "She's gonna blow!"

The rumbling got louder and louder as the creature writhed, expanding from the selenium.

- - -

A mile away, Flemming watched the scene through his binoculars. "Dear Lord," he said.

- - -

Meanwhile, back at the giant amoeba, Harry was still holding the hose inside the, writhing, expanding creature. "Well," he said to Ira, "I've seen about all there is to see. . . . How 'bout you?"

"How're we doing?" Ira called down to the Donalds.

"Almost there," yelled Deke, at the pumps. "Go!"

"Hit the ladder!" Ira yelled to Wayne. Wayne pulled back the lever, and the ladder began retracting.

"Allison! Get us outta here!" Ira yelled into the walkie-talkie.

Immediately, she hit the gas, making a wide U-turn and heading back toward the gap between the tentacles. The creature was growing and shaking and splitting, all at the same time.

The race was on. The hook-and-ladder sped toward the gap while the creature expanded, its surface bubbling and welting. The ground was shaking crazily. Harry and Ira held on for dear life.

Then, just as the fire truck shot out of the gap between the tentacles . . .

BOOOOOMMMM!

The amoeba burst into a million parts, and all of a sudden it was raining big chunks of dead alien all over the place. A large, disgusting piece barely missed the speeding fire truck.

● ● ●

At the control center, Woodman looked up. "Uh-oh," he said, just before an enormous blob of smelly, gloppy alien gunk landed directly on the tent, covering everyone inside.

● ● ●

Our six heroes whooped and hollered jubilantly as they watched the dead alien amoeba crap pour down across the desert.

CHAPTER SEVENTEEN

Later that night, the compound, or what was left of it, was abuzz with activity. Soldiers broke down the tents, carted away equipment, and mopped up.

Woodman had to be hosed down by a couple of army privates.

And later still, our six heroes, battered, bruised, and covered in Head and Shoulders, but looking triumphant, stood behind Governor Lewis as he held a press conference.

"The president just called me personally," said the governor, leaning into the mikes, "to offer his thanks and best wishes—helluva guy—and now, without further ado, I'd like to introduce our civilian scientists and their team, the best the great state of Arizona has to offer. These brave souls risked life and limb to deliver the lethal selenium cocktail that blew the hideous alien creature straight to hell." He swept his arm toward the group. "The Donald boys, Derek and Danny," he said, "straight-A students at Glen Canyon Community College . . ."

The Donald brothers stepped forward, flashbulbs going off all around them.

"Big moment, huh?" Allison whispered to Ira. "You're finally going to get the credit you deserve."

"It's very gratifying," said Ira.

"Wayne Gray, fully licensed firefighter . . ." the governor continued, with a private wink at Wayne. "I've got friends," he said.

Wayne came forward and waved to the cameras. "I'd like to dedicate this moment to all those who lost their lives in this battle," he announced. He raised his fist, shouting to the sky, "This one's for you, Barry Cartwright!"

Allison and Ira were still having their side conversation. "A very big moment," she was saying. "You wouldn't want to miss this for anything. Well, practically anything."

"Professor Harry Block," Governor Lewis went on, "noted geologist and the winningest women's volleyball coach in northern Arizona . . ."

"Thanks, Gov," said Harry. "We just took it one alien at a time and we were able to walk away with the W."

"And finally," Governor Lewis wound it up, "Doctors Allison Reed and Ira Kane."

He turned to present them, but they were nowhere to be found. The remaining team of four exchanged confused looks.

"I was told they were here, where the hell are they?" the governor barked at his aides.

Then Harry smiled. He leaned over to Wayne. "Looks like

Dr. Reed is in for a little Kane Madness," he said with a grin.

● ● ●

And indeed, Allison and Ira were at that moment in the front seat of the fire truck. They came up for air, their clothing totally rumpled, with huge smiles on their faces.

"Wow," said Ira. "When you say you're gonna rock someone's world, you really mean it."

"Well, you did fulfill a fantasy of mine," she said.

"You mean saving the world?"

"No," she said, "making out in a fire truck."

They both laughed. Now that the world wasn't going to end, they could move on to more exciting things.